A Tale of
False Fortunes

A Tale of False Fortunes

Enchi Fumiko

Translated by Roger K. Thomas

University of Hawai'i Press, Honolulu

Namamiko Monogatari by Enchi Fumiko © 1965
English translation rights arranged with the Estate of Enchi Fumiko
through The Wylie Agency, Inc.

English translation © 2000 University of Hawai'i Press
Printed in the United States of America
04 03 02   5 4 3 2

Library of Congress Cataloging-in-Publication Data
Enchi, Fumiko, 1905–
    [Namamiko monogatari. English]
    A tale of false fortunes / Enchi Fumiko ; translated
      by Roger K. Thomas.
        p.   cm.
    ISBN 0-8248-2135-1 (cloth : alk. paper) —
      ISBN 0-8248-2187-4 (pbk. : alk. paper)
    I. Title. II. Thomas, Roger Kent, 1953–
    PL826.N3 N313 2000
    895.6'35 21—dc21

                                99-046525

Publication of this book has been supported by a grant
from the Kajiyama Publication Fund for Japanese History,
Culture, and Literature at the University of Hawai'i.

University of Hawai'i Press books are printed on acid-free
paper and meet the guidelines for permanence and durability
of the Council on Library Resources.

Printed by The Maple-Vail Book Manufacturing Group

Contents ∽

Introduction ⌒

Enchi Fumiko (1905–1986), noted for her translation of *The Tale of Genji* into modern Japanese and for her encyclopedic knowledge of Japan's classics, commented in her later years that "the women of the Heian aristocracy all seem to be cast in the same mold" and that she did "not particularly like them," but that she was "rather fond of Fujiwara Teishi, the consort of Emperor Ichijō," whom she found to be "vivid and fresh" ("Teidan," 31). That her admiration of Teishi was genuine is amply evinced by her 1965 work, *A Tale of False Fortunes (Namamiko monogatari)*, in which she not only crafted an innovative form of historical fiction but also created a new image of womanhood through her portrayal of Teishi.

A Tale of False Fortunes is unquestionably Enchi's most ambitious work of historical fiction and, as winner of the fifth Women's Literature Prize (Joryū Bungaku-shō) in 1966, also arguably her best. In it, the author creates a textual foil to *A Tale of Flowering Fortunes (Eiga monogatari)*, the panegyric to Fujiwara no Michinaga (966–1028) written mainly by Akazome Emon, a lady-in-waiting to Michinaga's principal wife, Rinshi. Michinaga assumes almost god-like stature in Akazome's narrative, which describes a time when Fujiwara control of the throne was at its zenith. By making sure that every empress—and every dowager empress—was from a ranking Fujiwara family, the emperor was easily manipulated by male maternal relatives who, since early times in Japan, had exercised greater customary power than paternal kin. Moreover, emperors were pressured to retire young in order to prevent the experience and cumulative wisdom of age from defying the de facto power of the regency. In Enchi's recreation of Michinaga's machinations to realize his ambitions, a challenge comes from an unforeseen source and in an unexpected form.

Throughout *A Tale of False Fortunes* a fictional document is cited as the "source" of Enchi's portrayal of Teishi and of the events surrounding her life at court. This document, which Enchi professes to have perused often enough in her youth to have committed lengthy portions to memory, is cited throughout in extracts rendered in a convincing Heian-style prose, the production of which itself constitutes no mean achievement for a twentieth-century writer. (Apocryphal stories have circulated of attempts to find the lost "manuscript" cited in her story soon after its appearance.)

The plausibility of such a work existing among the books left to Enchi's father by Basil Chamberlain is weighed against the implausibility of even so perspicacious a mind as hers recalling long extracts verbatim after half a lifetime. The reader's mind is constantly engaged in making such judgments and is thus drawn into the story, alternately affirming or denying the veracity of the source document, or of Enchi's narrative based thereon. This fictitious document offers an alternative account to that appearing in *A Tale of Flowering Fortunes*. Enchi frequently interjects her own "suppositions" about the fictive document, lending it an aura of credibility. In mixing real historical sources with a fictive one, she thus blends "what was" with "what might have happened" in a convincing and natural manner.

Enchi herself acknowledged that she got the idea of building a narrative around a fictitious historical document from reading Tanizaki Jun'ichirō's "A Portrait of Shunkin" (Shunkin shō; Enchi 1986, 193). Moreover, certain instances of sensual fixation in Enchi's work—like that of Yukikuni for Teishi in the latter part of the novel—are also redolent of Tanizaki's fiction (Kamei and Ogasawara, 77). Like "A Portrait of Shunkin," there are three levels of narrative language in *A Tale of False Fortunes:* extracts from the alleged document, a reconstructed story based thereon, and the author's own commentary. There are at least as many differences as similarities, however, in the way the spurious document is used in the story. First, the setting of Tanizaki's work was close to his own time, and cannot be considered historical fiction. Moreover, his "commentary" is far more limited, confined for the most part to the beginning and end; Enchi, on the other hand, interjects her comments throughout, and even offers her speculations on the reliability of the source. The most important difference, however, is perhaps that Tanizaki did not use the fictitious document as an "alternative" account to an existing historical source.

Enchi elsewhere experimented with narrative structures involving a fabricated document. "An Account of the Shrine in the Fields"—an alleged "study" that offers an alternative perspective on spirit possession in *The Tale of Genji*—is cited in full in her 1958 novel, *Masks (Onnamen)*, where it provides a backdrop for the theme of shamanism in that work. Enchi herself appears as a character in her outstanding 1965 work, *The Doll Sisters (Ningyō shimai)*, in which she attempts to unravel the enigma presented by Ritsuko's diary, likewise a fictional document that creates a tension between verisimilitude and implausibility. Rather than viewing this technique as imitative of Tanizaki, it is perhaps more accurate to see the works of both writers as telling examples of the persistent tendency in Japanese literature to balance seeming "fact" and fantasy. This tendency is idealized in Chikamatsu Monzaemon's (1653–1724) famous dictum characterizing art as lying "in the slender margin between the real and the unreal," and is cited by J. Thomas Rimer as one of the "Four Polarities" (that of Fiction/Fact) characterizing enduring traits in Japanese literature (Rimer, 15–20).

Readers familiar with Enchi's fiction will recognize certain traits Teishi holds in common with other heroines in her works, whether the finally unyielding determination of Shirakawa Tomo in *The Waiting Years (Onnazaka)* (1955) or the disarming, mediumistic mystique of Kanzaki Chigako in *Enchantress (Yō)* (1956) and Toganō Mieko in *Masks*. Like these, Teishi possesses an inner strength that proves ultimately to be an insurmountable challenge to men cast in adversarial roles.

And yet, Teishi is different from the others in some very important respects. While Chigako is preoccupied with aging and with her declining beauty, the years of illness and hardship only add to Teishi's charm. Hers is purely a "moral victory," one achieved entirely without scheming. It is not a deep resentment that fuels her strength, but rather the power of her undeviating love for and devotion to the emperor, and her "victory" over Michinaga does not involve rancor or malice toward anyone. The contrast with Tomo's bitterness, which in the end congealed into a core of resentment hard enough to "split . . . [Yukitomo's] arrogant ego in two" (Enchi 1971, 203), or with Mieko's and Chigako's calculating manipulation, could hardly be more striking. In response to Yoshida Seiichi's comment that it was "unusual for an ideal type of woman to appear" in Enchi's works, Enchi conceded that "most of them are rather spiteful," but that "comparatively speaking [Teishi] is not like that" (Enchi 1986, 21).

The creation of a convincing story of true love is singularly difficult in this cynical age, and the fact that a writer often charged with misandry should have attempted and succeeded at such a feat is truly extraordinary. Enchi's success in this daunting venture no doubt is due in no small measure to the unusual narrative technique that she employed (Takenishi, 168), as well as perhaps to the fact that its setting is available to us only through the imagination. As noted previously, the narrative structure itself attempts to evoke skepticism and credibility in each of its three components. What Enchi hoped to achieve through such a technique is yet another speculation that the work is likely to elicit in the minds of thoughtful readers. A host of different answers might be offered to such a question, but one worthy of noting here is the possibility that "a mutually satisfying love relationship" like that described as existing between Teishi and Emperor Ichijō "is something that can only be imagined in a 'false' *(nama)*, classical-age *monogatari*," and that in such a light, *A Tale of False Fortunes* "becomes not an alternative to but a supporting document for the gnarled view of relations between the sexes described in *The Waiting Years* and *Masks*" (Gessel, 384). For Enchi, true love belonged to the realm of historical imagination.

It has been argued that *A Tale of False Fortunes* represents a third and "final stage" in the quest for female empowerment, one in which "Enchi tired of conventional realism and began exploring the world of myth and fantasy, producing texts in which the antirational and the transtemporal were the norm" (Hulvey, 215). For Enchi, the world of fantasy appears to have been more accommodating to a depiction of love, but just as the narrative of this work maintains an equilibrium between doubt and belief, fantasy is likewise everywhere balanced against a compelling sense of realism. One realistic feature of *A Tale of False Fortunes* is its convincing portrayal of men, a notable contrast to the often caricatured or stock male figures in such works as *The Waiting Years* or *Masks*.

The structure of Enchi's narrative has been described as tripartite: the fictitious document, the account as recorded in an existing source *(A Tale of Flowering Fortunes),* and the author's own commentary. When one considers the role played by spirit possession *(mono no ke)* in the development of the narrative, the structure is arguably quadripartite, because here also the text creates a balance in the reader's mind between doubt and credulity.

Spirit possession is a ubiquitous presence in Heian literature. A medium voicing the resentment of a departed person's spirit *(shiryō)* is common to many cultures, but less familiar is possession by the "living ghosts" *(ikiryō)* of those still in this life who may be quite unaware of the hauntings by their spirits. Unplaced spirits on either side of the grave could wreak havoc, but significantly, both the possessed and the possessor were most often female. The function of spirit possession "within the politics of Heian polygynous society" has been cogently interpreted "as a predominantly female strategy adopted to counter male strategies of empowerment" (Bargen, xix). Through much of *A Tale of False Fortunes,* even this female strategy is appropriated by Michinaga to further his own ambitions until Teishi thwarts his plans with what is ostensibly an actual possession, one motivated not by resentment but by genuine love. The balance between the believability and implausibility of such a possession occurs within a larger balance: Enchi's reconstructed text as historical or fictive. Thus, in "Enchi Fumiko's fictional adaptation of Heian supernatural material . . . spirit possession functions both as plot line and as critical reflection or metafictional discourse" (Bargen, 304), enriching the narrative with yet another dimension.

Miko (female shamans) and mediumistic women are a perennial presence in much of Enchi's fiction, and it has been argued that her "fascination with *miko* is related to her desire to recapture the empowered role played by women in Japanese history" (Hulvey, 193). However, this interest in spiritualist powers appears not to have operated consciously in her writing. In response to Nakagami Kenji's comment that her works contain a mediumistic element *(miko-teki na mono)*, Enchi said: "I myself do not feel that there is a mediumistic element. I am often labeled [as being preoccupied] with female vindictiveness or karma, but I myself do not really see that. I suppose it might be there subconsciously" (Enchi 1986, 177).

In introducing a work like this to a Western audience, it seems appropriate to give an accounting of what is unavoidably lost in translation. Most regrettably in the present case, the distinction between Enchi's prose in modern Japanese and her unusually adept rendering of Heian-style language is here necessarily leveled into undifferentiated modern English, and this detracts in no small measure from its effectiveness in maintaining the balance between verisimilitude and unbelievability that is so essential to the working of the narrative. The possibility of rendering the "ancient" passages into archaic English was considered, but since a pre-Chaucerian style would be necessary in order to approximate the degree of difference in the original, I felt the result might be uninviting to readers. In an attempt to compensate visually and psychologically for what has been lost stylistically, a contrasting typeface has been used for the passages from Enchi's "source" document. I have also endeavored to employ a perceptibly dissimilar style in translating these sections. Further, the rendition of the complex system of honorifics found in the speech of Heian courtiers into English—that most democratic of tongues—inevitably results in an effect palpably different from the original, and I can only hope that my attempts sound neither stilted nor too demotic.

For translations of ranks and titles, I am indebted to William

H. and Helen Craig McCullough's usages in their translation of *A Tale of Flowering Fortunes,* the historical source to which Enchi's work is intended to provide an alternative perspective. To emphasize the intended parallelism between the two works, I have rendered the title as *A Tale of False Fortunes,* although "A Tale of False Oracles" or "A Tale of a False Shaman" would have been more literal. I wish to take this occasion to thank the two anonymous readers of the University of Hawai'i Press for their thoughtful criticism and constructive suggestions.

R. K. T.

Sources

Bargen, Doris G. *A Woman's Weapon: Spirit Possession in the The Tale of Genji.* Honolulu: University of Hawai'i Press, 1997.

Enchi Fumiko. *The Waiting Years.* Trans. John Bester. Tokyo: Kodansha International, 1971.

Enchi Fumiko. *Uen no hitobito to: Taidanshū.* Tokyo: Bungei Shunjū, 1986.

Gessel, Van. "The 'Medium' of Fiction: Fumiko Enchi as Narrator." *World Literature Today* (1988): 380–385.

Hulvey, S. Yumiko. "The Intertextual Fabric of Narratives by Enchi Fumiko." In *Japan in Traditional and Postmodern Perspectives.* Ed. Charles Wei-hsun Fu and Steven Heine. Albany: State University Press of New York, 1995, 169–224.

Kamei Hideo and Ogasawara Yoshiko. *Enchi Fumiko no sekai.* Tokyo: Sōrinsha, 1981.

McCullough, William H., and Helen Craig McCullough, trans. *A Tale of Flowering Fortunes: Annals of Japanese Aristocratic Life in the Heian Period.* 2 vols. Stanford: Stanford University Press, 1980.

Rimer, J. Thomas. "Japanese Literature: Four Polarities." *Japanese Aesthetics and Culture: A Reader.* Ed. Nancy G. Hume. Albany: State University of New York Press, 1995, 1–25.

Takenishi Hiroko. "Namamiko monogatari ron." *Tenbō* (Jan. 1976): 162–171.

"Teidan: kyūtei saijo no miryoku." *Kyūtei o irodoru saijo.* Ed. Tsubota Itsuo. Nihon hakken jinbutsu shiriizu 12. Tokyo: Akatsuki Kyōiku Tosho, 1983, 29–36.

Historical Figures in *A Tale of False Fortunes*

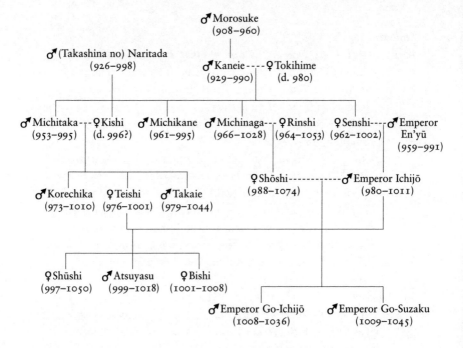

Prologue ~

When I was young, I knew Dr. Basil Hall Chamberlain by the name "Mr. Chamberlain." Of course, I had not actually seen him, but I had become accustomed to hearing the name "Mr. Chamberlain" interspersed in my father's conversations. My father, who had formerly studied philology under Dr. Chamberlain, always spoke of him casually as Mr. Chamberlain, in much the same fashion as university students even now refer to their professors behind their backs.

I was probably six years old when my young ears committed Dr. Chamberlain's name to memory. I am able to recall my exact age because that year we had moved from Fujimi in Kōji-machi to Yanaka Shimizu in Shitaya, and upstairs in our new house there were tall stacks of old books I had never seen before. For some time, scholars acquainted with my father and people from newspaper offices made frequent visits for the purpose of examining those tomes. Now as I commence writing, I open the *Encyclopedia of Japanese Literature,* where I find the following entry on Chamberlain:

> Basil Hall Chamberlain. Philologist. Born 1850 in Portsmouth, England. Died Feb. 15, 1935, at the age of 86. As a child he studied languages at a school in Versailles, France, and grew up aspiring to literature. . . . Illness resulted from excessive study and, on the advice of a doctor, he set out on a long ocean cruise. He arrived in Tokyo, where he devoted himself to research in Japanese literature. . . . In 1886, at the invitation of the Ministry of Education, he became a lecturer in the College of Humanities at the Imperial University, where he taught Japanese language and philology. In 1890, he resigned because of illness, and

returned to England. . . . After that he made frequent trips to Japan and continued his research. In 1910 he made his last research trip, and bade farewell to nearly forty years of living in Japan. . . . Over many years, he had collected 11,000 volumes of rare and unusual books in Japanese and Chinese, known as the Ōdō Library. Upon his departure for England, he considered it unbecoming for a scholar to take this collection to Europe, where there were few who would be able to use it, and gave the entire library to Ueda Kazutoshi. Such an act stands as eloquent testimony of his character.

As we see here, Dr. Chamberlain's final stay in Japan was in 1910. It was probably 1911 by the time the library was put in order and moved into my father's house, or about the time we moved. If my mother, who died last year in her eighties, were here I could verify the date, but there are few among my acquaintances now who clearly recall those times.

Dr. Chamberlain's books bore a red stamp in large, square characters: "Ōdō Library." I had heard so few anecdotes about Dr. Chamberlain from my father that it was not until I consulted the *Encyclopedia of Japanese Literature* that I learned "Ōdō" (King Hall) was a Japanization of Chamberlain's own name—"Basil" from Greek *basileus,* or king.

And so I ended up not knowing what sort of "rare and unusual books" the Ōdō Library contained, but even now I clearly recall as a child, when I would go upstairs, seeing in my father's study Japanese-style lidded book boxes made of unfinished wood and piles upon piles of old books in the sunlit area of the narrow, tatami-matted hallway. Most of them, of course, were stitch-bound books printed on light Japanese paper or handwritten texts in beautiful, flowing cursive. As a child I could not very well read such characters, so I looked at them with a curiosity peculiar to children—a strange blend of scorn and reverence—much like what I felt at seeing the contents of an old-fashioned wardrobe chest. From summer into autumn, I would dash about the parlor among books set out with their pages open for airing, and sometimes I would even try leafing through a worm-eaten volume. But when I was in the upper level of grammar school and had learned to read the old cursive syllabary at calligraphy lessons, my browsing turned into reading as I carefully followed each line of characters in books written in understandable styles of script.

The story that I propose to write now is from one of the handwritten books I read in this manner upstairs in my father's house; however, relying only on the uncertain memory of my childhood, I cannot say whether it was one of the "rare and unusual" books of the Ōdō Library. It was possibly one of my father's own books that just happened to get mixed in with the Ōdō Library. At any rate, no matter whom I asked later, no one had heard of it. Judging from that, the story must have been a transcription of an older book from the Kamakura or Muromachi period, or possibly a fictional work by a not-so-famous literary scholar of the Tokugawa period—perhaps a second-rate work by Takebe Ayatari.

It was forty years ago, and many details of the book's appearance now escape me. I am certain, however, that a rectangular strip of thick vellum speckled with gold and silver was mounted on the left side of its cover of navy blue Japanese paper, and that on the vellum, written in somewhat blurred *Man'yō* script in the style of the Heian-period calligrapher Fujiwara no Yukinari, was this: *A Tale of False Fortunes*. What were the "false fortunes"? Goaded by the curiosity these strange words aroused, I opened to the title page, where the title appeared again in running cursive followed by the subtitle: *Gleanings from "A Tale of Flowering Fortunes."* Only upon seeing the Chinese characters used in the inside title did I realize that the book was about a spirit medium.

A Tale of False Fortunes tells of the life of a lady-in-waiting in service to the consort of Emperor Ichijō. A young girl reader like myself was naturally interested in the stormy fate of the heroine, and I plowed through the difficult cursive writing, reading it over and over until I understood it. Much later, when out of some necessity I read *A Tale of Flowering Fortunes* in the anthology of classics edited by Yosano Akiko and others, I noticed that some of the passages I had read long ago in *A Tale of False Fortunes* had been borrowed intact from the more famous work. By that time my father had already died and his library had passed into another's possession, and I had no way of determining the whereabouts of the original manuscript of *A Tale of False Fortunes*. In all probability, however, that one volume was the sole copy. But the reason I took it into my head to compare the two works was not because *False Fortunes* quotes many passages intact from *Flowering Fortunes,* but rather because things not found in the latter appear in the former; in other words, because of what is summed up in the subtitle: *Gleanings from "A Tale of Flowering Fortunes."*

It is well known that the principal part of *A Tale of Flowering Fortunes* was written by Akazome Emon, who served Shōshi (daughter of Fujiwara no Michinaga), the second consort of Emperor Ichijō. Akazome was the wife of the noted Sinologist and poet Ōe no Masahira. Her reputation also as a poet is attested by the comparison, in Murasaki Shikibu's diary, of Izumi Shikibu's poems with those of Akazome, where Murasaki judged the latter to be superior. But Akazome's temperament was unlike the purely literary dispositions of Izumi Shikibu, Sei Shōnagon, or Murasaki Shikibu; Akazome must have been more of a commonsensical sort of person who was also endowed with literary talent. From the prosaic nature of the narration in *A Tale of Flowering Fortunes* and from the fact that Akazome would borrow passages intact from other writers to aid in her own narrative (her description of Michinaga's residence at the time Shōshi's first child was born was borrowed from the *Murasaki Shikibu Diary*), we may see that she did not possess the strongly individualistic character typical of most writers, and that rather than putting a premium on her own style, she was by nature a researcher who attached greatest importance to the accuracy of her descriptions.

And then, too, in one respect *A Tale of Flowering Fortunes* is also a genealogy—a eulogistic hymn, as it were—of the Fujiwara family, written with the purpose of giving greater glory to the life of the regent Michinaga. It therefore shows a strong tendency to look with indifference on those who opposed Michinaga and, of course, to omit descriptions that otherwise ought to have been recorded. Just by comparing it with a historical romance like *The Great Mirror*, whose author is thought to have been a man, the extent to which Akazome views things from the position of Michinaga becomes evident. In her writing, the closer the narrative comes to Michinaga's age, the more it loses its comprehensive historical view.

Perhaps the author of *A Tale of False Fortunes* had these same impressions upon reading *A Tale of Flowering Fortunes*. Aided perhaps by a knowledge of the history of the Monarchical Age and by something of a chivalrous spirit in siding with those who suffered defeats and setbacks, the author of *False Fortunes* must have intended to show the other side of things, borrowing passages here and there from the earlier work.

That my inference is not merely arbitrary is born out by the fact that the content of *A Tale of False Fortunes* is quite different in tone from the eulogistic hymn to the regent's family. *False Fortunes* attempts instead to portray by contrast the victor's tyranny hidden behind his prosperity and the sudden misfortunes and ruin of those who attempted to resist that tyranny. The story was written either in the Kamakura period—not long after the Monarchical Age—or in the Tokugawa period by a writer of the pseudoclassicist school. I am certain that the manuscript I saw was not so very old, but I am unable to determine for sure whether or not it was the original copy. The date of this story's composition thus remains vague. If, based on this description, the original copy of *A Tale of False Fortunes* should turn up somewhere, there could be nothing more gratifying. But barring that possibility—and considering that my life is half over and that my memory is rapidly deteriorating—there may be some value in my recording for posterity the contents of *A Tale of False Fortunes*, a work no one but myself seems to have read and that I have committed to fairly accurate memory. I shall fill in gaps by referring to *A Tale of Flowering Fortunes* and other documents.

Of course, if by chance the real *Tale of False Fortunes* should show up somewhere, a close comparison will no doubt reveal many errors in what I write here. After the passage of nearly forty years, the things I read in books as a child or saw in plays blend with the gamut of emotions experienced in real life and are woven together into a single entity within me that is difficult to separate from reality, and that takes on an elusive life of its own.

However, my decision to call up this story from memory and to reconstruct it with the aid of early histories owes to a fortuitous meeting in Geneva, Switzerland, on a recent trip abroad. I learned that Dr. Chamberlain had spent his later years in seclusion there.

The source of this information was a young man, proficient in English, who worked in a watch shop on a main road near Lake Leman. Because of the kimono I was wearing at the time, he perceived immediately that I was Japanese and made some amiable conversation after the sale. He mentioned the name of Dr. Chamberlain, who had been laid to rest there over twenty years ago. Of course, the shop clerk had not known the professor personally, but said that his mother had gone to assist with housekeeping at the professor's residence and had received such things as a Japanese cloth (probably a *furoshiki*) and a doll. I asked about the professor's wife and children, but he knew nothing of them. After having mentioned this British philologist to many Japanese and having met only with indifferent reactions, the young man seemed rather gratified that I knew something of the professor.

Naturally, when I heard him speak Dr. Chamberlain's name, I, too, could not help feeling that it was a strangely coincidental meeting.

When I completed my purchase and left the shop, the young man followed after me and, pointing to an area beyond the bridge, said: "On the other side of the Mont Blanc Bridge over there is a landing for an excursion boat. I was told that Professor Chamberlain would sit on a bench every day on the water's edge and look out over the lake there. Even rain never prevented him from coming for a walk with a cane in one hand and an umbrella in the other."

Following the young man's directions, I crossed the Mont Blanc Bridge and walked along the lakefront, turning down a street lined with hotels. The excursion boat was docked at the landing, and I could see several people who looked like tourists descending the wide staircase of the landing in order to board the boat. It was a lightly overcast afternoon toward the end of June, but the air had an autumnal chill about it, and the women of the town all looked warm walking about in thick woolen waistcoats. Here and there were flower beds planted with small blooms in patterns like carpets. The colors of the flowers, like the colors of the townswomen's clothing, were of a sober tone, mellow and warm, which, combined with the cold impression given by the people's Nordic features, eloquently bespoke the characteristic harmony and sense of proportion possessed by the Swiss nation. Absent was a sense of the inscrutable charm of frenzied passion or of confusion; instead, an ultimate miniaturization of human happiness seemed to be preserved there more than anywhere else in the world.

I sat down on the bench closest to the lake, gazing at the graceful, veil-like spray of the tall jet of water from a fountain on the other side and at the outline of the peak of Mont Blanc, dimly visible in the distance. It occurred to me that the color of the waters of Lake Leman and the imposing shape of Mont Blanc before me now were probably not so very different from what the old philologist saw more than twenty years ago as he walked here daily with his cane and sat on a bench on the lakeside. Such musing moved me to reminiscence. I have no way of knowing what has happened to the thousands of books Dr. Chamberlain left in Japan in the hopes that they would be used by Japanese. Are they now in a library somewhere, or in a private collection? At any rate, it was then that *A Tale of False Fortunes*, which may have been one of those books, sprang back to life in my mind. I determined then that when I returned to Japan, I would write it down, comparing what I remember of the story with *A Tale of Flowering Fortunes*.

Chapter One ~

If my memory is not mistaken, the opening section of *A Tale of False Fortunes* consists largely of extracts from chapters of the first volume of *A Tale of Flowering Fortunes* and chronicles the struggle for power in the regency after the death of Michinaga's father, Fujiwara no Kaneie. In describing the refinement of the heroine's life, it was no doubt necessary to portray as its background the tragedy of an aristocratic society caught in the internecine feuds of the age. Those descriptions are taken almost intact from *A Tale of Flowering Fortunes*, and I, too, shall begin by recounting them. I distinctly recall that *A Tale of False Fortunes* opened with the following words:

> *During the reign of Emperor Ichijō, there were two consorts. The first of these was Fujiwara no Teishi, the daughter of the Regent Michitaka. Thereafter came Fujiwara no Shōshi, the eldest daughter of the Buddha-Hall Lord (Michinaga). Also known as Jōtōmon'in, Shōshi was the mother of Emperors Go-Ichijō and Go-Suzaku.*

This account is, of course, not found in *A Tale of Flowering Fortunes*, a history of the court from early Heian times focusing on the Fujiwara family.

I do not recall the extent to which abbreviated text from *Flowering Fortunes* was used in the succeeding sections, but I am certain that the narrative began from the time when the Higashisanjō chancellor, Kaneie, was still alive and his eldest son, the palace minister Michitaka, had his eldest daughter Teishi installed in court as junior consort to the still-youthful emperor. I, too, shall interpolate descriptions of what I remember from *False Fortunes* as I give a free rendition of portions of the earlier work. This kind of writing amounts to a sort of cut-and-paste work, rather irritating to one like me who is used to writing fiction, but there is no other way to reconstruct *A Tale of False Fortunes* in a manner that would be a credit to the story—a story that remains nowhere but in my memory.

On the fifth day of the first month of Shōryaku 1 (990), the Coming-of-Age Ceremony was performed for the emperor (Ichijō). He was still a youth of eleven years, and there were those who lamented, remarking that his childhood and the charm of his boyish attire were now things of the past. Even with his hair bound up and a man's cap set on his head, however, he looked very trim and splendid in spite of his small stature.

In the second month, the palace minister Michitaka presented his eldest daughter in court, and both the palace and the minister's own household were bustling with preparations for the ceremonies. Michitaka's wife, Kishi, was well versed in the ways of the court, having served there under the name Kō no Naishi. She much preferred a modish and resplendent style over solemn, esoteric matters, and her tastes were reflected in her arrangements for her daughter's presentation at court. The young woman had just turned sixteen, five years older than the emperor. That same evening after the ceremonies, she assumed the position of junior consort.

Shortly thereafter, Kaneie fell ill. Michitaka, the emperor's mother (Kaneie's daughter Senshi), and others among the nobles were distraught with worry. Incantations and prayers on behalf of the chancellor were performed everywhere throughout the land, but he showed no sign of recovery. His residence, Nijōin, was infested with the evil spirits that had always haunted the family of Lord Kujō (Morosuke). To these were added the vengeful spirits of both the living and the dead who bore resentment toward Kaneie. Taking advantage of his weakened state, these malevolent spirits contrived to obstruct prayers offered on his behalf. Even the spiritual powers of famous priests like the chief abbot of Hieizan availed nothing against the evil spirits. The women called in as mediums looked like specters themselves, their faces ghastly pallid, their eyes twitching, and their hair disheveled. The priests performing the exorcisms whipped the women with rosaries, attempting to prostrate them, but they rolled about and jumped up in defiance. The mediums were both laughing and weeping, and the resulting confusion was like a scene from hell itself. An especially dreadful one among them was possessed by the vengeful ghost of Emperor Murakami's daughter, the third princess, of whom Kaneie had been enamored in his youth. He had soon tired of her and left her, for which cause she was made the object of much gossip and was despised at court. She became despondent and grieved herself to death.

The medium, known as Ayame of Miwa, was the daughter of the priestess of Miwa. Although ordinarily a timid, inarticulate young woman, while possessed she assumed the lofty mien of the princess herself and denounced Kaneie's coldness and cruelty. The intrepid Kaneie, who appeared not to have been particularly intimidated by the imprecations and reproaches of other evil spirits, was deeply shaken by the specter of the third princess. The young court noble most like Kaneie in temperament was his own youngest son, the lesser commander of the guards (Michinaga), whom Kaneie is said to have warned sternly: "There are all kinds of transgressions in this world, but make sure you are never guilty of giving a woman cause for resentment. At first it may remain unexpressed, and you will put it out of your mind with no thought of consequences. But I'm afraid that even if I tell you how horrible those unexpressed resentments can become, someone your age would probably not understand."

Under these circumstances, Kaneie's daughter (the emperor's mother) and sons repeatedly urged him to change residences. He obliged and moved to the Higashisanjō mansion, but the evil spirits followed him there and his condition only grew worse. On the fifth day of the fifth month he resigned from the positions of chancellor and regent, and a few days later took religious orders. An imperial proclamation was immediately issued appointing the palace minister, Michitaka, as regent.

Though it was perhaps only natural for Kaneie's eldest son to receive such an appointment, news of it pitched the Higashi-sanjō mansion into such a state of agitation that it seemed almost as if Kaneie's illness had been forgotten. Those of that household as well as people in other prominent families naturally watched with raised brows as Michitaka's father-in-law and brothers-in-law—men who were not even of Fujiwara lineage—went swaggering about as if they owned the place. The new regent himself seemed to go along with the inveigling of those around him who wanted his daughter to be elevated from junior consort to empress as soon as possible. This was accomplished on the first day of the sixth month. There was gossip about the new regent: he was able to steer everything to his advantage, but his actions were unfeeling and indiscreet in light of his father's grave illness. Furthermore, what did he have in mind by appointing the lesser commander of the guards, an uncle to the empress, as steward of the empress' household? Did he think Michinaga's broad-mindedness about everything would afford the right protection for his daughter? If that was what Michitaka was thinking, then he was an unusually gullible sort of person, unable to see the bold ambition lurking behind his youngest brother's magnanimous demeanor.

As might be expected, the position of steward of the empress' household seemed of little interest to Michinaga, and he had not even properly paid his respects at the palace before Kaneie passed away on the second day of the seventh month. It appeared that matters of government would now proceed exactly as the new regent desired, and that the other nobles would have no recourse but to follow his directives. Michinaga could not go on indefinitely neglecting his duties as steward of the empress' household, so he would occasionally make an appearance and offer some solicitous advice, all the while keeping a keenly observant eye on the condition of the empress and the deportment of the ladies-in-waiting.

Now this Michinaga, the most handsome in his family, was highly regarded among the ladies-in-waiting, who were wont to say that his combination of masculine manners and refinement was unusual even among the young nobles. Of all his brothers, Michinaga was also the favorite of the emperor's mother. It was only natural, then, that he should come to be on familiar terms with some of the ladies-in-waiting as he frequented the palace of the new empress, and he paid close attention to her manners and appearance as he disported himself with her women. Michinaga himself had a beautiful daughter who, though still young, showed much promise. Not too many years hence, she would arrive at an age compatible with that of the emperor, and Michinaga sought a model in the present empress' rise to renown.

The new empress had inherited her mother's remarkably intelligent nature and was so accomplished—whether in poetry, calligraphy, *koto*, or lute—that even men who were thought to be very proficient did not surpass her. And yet she made no ostentatious display of her talents. Her engaging but graceful demeanor had an indescribable elegance about it, like combining the scent of plum blossoms with the sight of the spring's first cherry blossoms.

When Teishi was made junior consort, the emperor at first thought he might be shy with an older woman. No sooner had he entered the bedchamber, though, than he was at her side making casual bedtime conversation about old tales and events. Her manners were different from the matronly, experienced bearing of his nurses, and her entire body was of slender build: smooth, supple, and indescribably charming. Her lithe movements, like the pliant bending of a willow twig, captivated the heart of the youth in a vaguely unsettling way.

Ben's and Tayū's bosoms are ample, as if they had placed great bowls on their chests, but the Empress' breasts are a cold roundness, like the buds of a white peony tinged with crimson. I delight in sleeping with my cheek in her bosom.

When his majesty's unabashed words were obligingly divulged to Michinaga by a lady-in-waiting, the thought sprang into his mind: surely the empress must be without equal.

Retired emperor En'yū passed away in the second month of the following year, not long after having received a visit from his son, Emperor Ichijō, who had sought his counsel on government. The retired emperor was reassured by his son's appearance, which had grown even more strikingly handsome since his Coming-of-Age Ceremony. Actually, En'yū was not of so advanced an age that he needed to have abdicated so soon in favor of his son, but the late chancellor (Kaneie) had been anxious to have his own grandchild, the crown prince, enthroned as soon as possible. En'yū relinquished the throne, feeling that circumstances militated against his continued reign. Perhaps, too, he wished to spend his remaining years at peace with the thought that he had shored up the crown prince's future reign before retiring.

As things were, the passing of the retired emperor could only bring greater prosperity to the new regent's household. The regent's father-in-law, Naritada, a lay priest, was elevated to second rank and was widely acclaimed as the "Novice of the Second Rank" or as senior second rank. Though he was advanced in years, his learning and abilities seemed to know no limits. He was strong-minded and difficult to deal with, and some had misgivings about him. Many were also disturbed to see the brothers of the regent's wife all given appointments as governors of provinces, though they were hardly of a birth that would make them worthy of such distinctions. There was no dearth of criticisms: "What an awful state of affairs! One can only hope that no unrest comes from this."

Having written this far, one thing that occurs to me is that *A Tale of Flowering Fortunes* contains almost no praise of the appearance and talent of Empress Teishi, daughter of Regent Michitaka. Many such accounts included here are therefore taken from the text of *A Tale of False Fortunes*.

My childhood impression of Empress Teishi as unusually beautiful and talented was based on descriptions in *A Tale of False Fortunes*, but later when I read *The Pillow Book*, I found passages throughout where Sei Shōnagon wrote in adulation of her. The image of the empress based on my earlier reading thus began to shine even more resplendently.

The following account appears in *The Pillow Book*:

In front of the bamboo blinds of the Empress' quarters, a group of nobles had spent the day making music with the flute and *koto*. The lattice had not yet been lowered when it was time for the lamps to be lit. The lamps were brought in, making the interior as plainly visible as if the door were open. The Empress was holding her lute lengthwise. She was dressed in a scarlet robe with several layered undergarments of glossy, pounded silk, the beauty of which defies description. It was a wonderful scene to see her sleeve draped over the jet black, glossy lute she was holding. Moreover, the contrast of the dazzling whiteness of her forehead as seen from the side was an incomparable sight to behold. I approached one of the women sitting nearby and said: "That woman with her face half hidden could not have been so beautiful. And she was a commoner." The woman pressed through the many people gathered about, and reported to the Empress what I had said. The Empress laughed, saying: "Does she know the meaning of parting?" I found it very amusing when her words were relayed back to me.

Sei Shōnagon's comparison alluded to the passage in Po Chü-i's "Song of the Lute" where the poet sent for a lute-playing woman in a boat: "Only after repeated entreaties did she come, / Her face half hidden by the lute she clutched." This incident probably took place when the regent's household—that of the empress' parents—was at the height of its prosperity. Even after Teishi's family's decline, however, when her life was abject and lonely save for the emperor's love, Sei Shōnagon's descriptions never failed to endow her mistress with the abundant beauty of a flower that never fades. Such praises of course bespeak Sei Shōnagon's own strong-mindedness, but Empress Teishi's perspicacious nature no doubt was also all the more finely honed as she sensed the impending, tragic decline of her parents' family and their fall from political power. Her unusual comeliness perhaps indeed shone all the more brilliantly in her later years.

In light of the fact that Teishi was the first woman presented to him at court, it is easily understandable that she remained Emperor Ichijō's favorite. For that very reason Michinaga kept a particularly vigilant eye on the empress, whom he saw as a future rival to his own daughter, though the latter was still of tender age. Teishi's father, Michitaka, was no match for Michinaga, in whose heart lay a deeply hidden bold ambition for power.

A Tale of Flowering Fortunes describes the various evil spirits that assailed Kaneie on his sickbed, but the name Ayame of Miwa, the medium who was possessed by the vengeful ghost of the third princess, appears only in *A Tale of False Fortunes*. Ayame of Miwa was the elder sister of Kureha of Miwa, the heroine of *A Tale of False Fortunes*. After Kaneie's death, Michinaga invited Ayame to become a lady-in-waiting in his own household.

Toyome, the mother of Ayame and Kureha, seemed to possess the greatest mediumistic powers among all of the shrine women serving the god of Kasuga, and it was she who usually received the oracle of the god. Now the god of Kasuga was the tutelary deity of the Fujiwara clan, whose members—including, of course, the head of the clan, the regent himself—made frequent pilgrimages. Toyome availed herself of one such occasion to offer Ayame to Regent Kaneie's household as a junior lady-in-waiting. After hearing Toyome pronounce an auspicious oracle, Kaneie was in good humor and agreed to take Ayame into his household.

As recorded in *A Tale of False Fortunes*, Toyome's words to Kaneie at that time were as follows:

> I am truly grateful that Your Lordship should grant the request of one so inept as I, and that you are willing to take Ayame into your service. Ayame is now fifteen years old, and her younger sister Kureha is only twelve. When Kureha is a few years older, I hope that she too might attend His Lordship's wife. If I can entrust my daughters to His Lordship, I shall have no worry about their future. But I should like to make just one request: I do not want them to work as mediums. I do not have them serve at this shrine because of this vow.
>
> For years now, I have been a mouthpiece for the gods

that have possessed my body, and I have pronounced words affecting important affairs of society as well as personal fortunes. But of course, I myself have never been conscious of any of those pronouncements. When I am possessed, a horrendous power weighs down on me and I become unable even to breathe, as if a huge rock were crushing me. At length I become unconscious of anything, and I never recall a single word I utter while in a trance. When I think about it, though, from time to time there have been frightening oracles from the gods: to do battle, or to take a person's life. I possessed no understanding of such matters, but I would realize later that important events to which I had never given thought had occurred as a result of the god's oracle through my mouth, and that has at times filled me with apprehension. At any rate, I am resigned to this as my own fate, but I do not want my daughters to follow in my path. Therefore, after Ayame enters your service, Your Lordship would be gravely mistaken to think that she possessed some knowledge of necromancy. I humbly beg you not to use her for work having to do with gods or spirits.

Behind Toyome's earnest entreaty to Kaneie was a secret that had been plaguing her.

Strictly speaking, shrine women were supposed to have remained virgins while in service to the gods, but in reality there were surprisingly many love affairs. It is perhaps reasonable to view the requirement of chastity as rooted more in a belief that the gods preferred a woman who was free to respond to a man's demands rather than in an abhorrence of female impurity.

In the "Emissary of Falconry" section of *The Tales of Ise*, the man appearing as Narihira called at the household of the Ise Virgin to pay his respects. While he was being entertained, he began to seek her affections. In the middle of that same night a woman accompanied by a serving girl appeared outside the bamboo blinds of his chamber. He invited the woman to enter, and who should come in but the virgin herself? Narihira made a pledge of love that night, but he set out early the next morning without being able to arrange another tryst with her. The serving girl brought a letter to him. He opened it to find only a poem written in the virgin's hand.

Kimi ya koshi	Did you come to me,
Ware ya yukikemu	Or was it I who went to you?
Omōezu	I cannot say—
Yume ka utsutsu ka	Was it dream or reality?
Nete ka samete ka.	Was I asleep or awake?

What we see here, then, is a noblewoman—an imperial princess and the virgin of the Ise Shrine, the highest-ranking shrine maiden in all the land—visiting Narihira's bedchamber of her own accord. Now of course *The Tales of Ise* are from the earliest stage of the Monarchical Age, and a good deal of rusticity even in the behavior of the nobility remained from the Nara period. Even allowing for that, an aggressiveness like that of a noblewoman in service to the gods calling on a man in his bedchamber is practically unheard of in other tales. Perhaps in the final analysis, although shrine maidens were not officially sanctioned to have affairs with mortal men aside from their devotions to the gods, such liaisons were tacitly permitted.

Viewed from one angle, a shrine maiden's state while possessed by a god also follows a course through extreme tension between body and mind, passing through ecstasy and finally to saturation. Through this course, the sex drives are naturally satisfied. In other words, a shrine maiden in a divine trance is performing a sort of sexual act. These women can be said to be liberated by the deity rather than confined by it. In this regard, there would seem to be a fundamental difference between the asceticism of Buddhist or Christian nuns and the shrine maidens of primitive Shinto. When their bodies are not being borrowed by a deity, shrine maidens harbor emotions much like those of young wives occupying lonely bedchambers while their husbands are away, their bodies seething with wild passions and replete with things that attract men.

Two reasons may be suggested to explain why Toyome's confessions were recounted in *A Tale of False Fortunes*. First, she had borne two daughters, Ayame and Kureha, as a result of this sort of "public secret." Second, the unexpected death of her lover was caused by none other than the words of the god that possessed her.

Toyome's lover, Usuki no Yoshinori, was a military officer in the service of the provincial governor.

In spite of having grown up in a military household, Yoshinori had a refined disposition and was accomplished at both writing and calculating. Should the opportunity present itself, therefore, he hoped to abandon his swords and secure a peaceful occupation—perhaps the stewardship in an influential nobleman's household or something like that. He was actually a rather unassertive man, and even the beginning of his love affair with Toyome apparently owed less to his own advances than to seduction by the untamed passion peculiar to shrine women. Yoshinori had promised Toyome that someday he would return to a settled life in the capital, that he would then take Toyome and their two daughters with him, and that they would all live in peace and harmony. However, his life was unexpectedly cut short through a singular occurrence, the circumstances of which are recorded thus in *A Tale of False Fortunes*:

> One year, many of the sacred deer in the precincts of Kasuga disappeared. Then children of merchant families turned up missing, and it was noised about that something suspicious was afoot. When the favorite serving girl of the governor's wife disappeared one night, the situation grew quite intolerable. A rigorous investigation was conducted throughout the entire province, but to no avail. Some said that there must be bandits hiding in the mountains, and places like Kazuraki and Yoshino were searched. When this yielded no leads, they determined for better or for worse to seek an oracle from the God of Kasuga. This command was delivered to the shrine, and the chief priest had Toyome purify herself and seek the God's oracle.
>
> As Toyome held up the offering of braided paper strips

and prayed, the God took possession of her body. Her face became pale, her eyes twitched, and she began to shake in a most frightening manner. After a while, a dreadful voice issued from her mouth: "The bandits who are stealing and eating my deer and taking my people's children are in the mountains of Ikoma. However, they will not be easy to destroy. The man to subdue them will have one large mole near his eye, and the middle finger of his right hand will be somewhat long. Make no mistake about this." After the God departed, the governor and all of the high officials reverently feared the oracle and searched Ikoma, where they found some bandits of truly strange appearance living in a cave deep in the mountains. Those outlaws did not even appear to be Japanese. Their hair was cut short, they had blue eyes, their faces were very ruddy, and they could run as fast as birds in flight.

Now then, according to the oracle of the God, the one to subdue these bandits could be none other than Usuki no Yoshinori. Near Yoshinori's left eye was a large mole, and the middle finger of his right hand was somewhat longer than that of his left. His comrades all knew that when he put his hands together, the right side was longer. They overwhelmingly chose Yoshinori in the belief that they would certainly subdue the bandits with him at their lead.

Yoshinori felt utterly wretched and tried many times to refuse, but the governor would not listen to his petition, and he was compelled to comply. Before setting out for Ikoma at the head of his troops, Yoshinori paid a visit to Kasuga. He finished worshiping, then turned to Toyome and said, weeping bitterly: "Because of an absurd, mistaken oracle, I now bear a miserable fate. I am not a powerful man, and in the end am not likely to return alive. Take good care of Ayame and Kureha. My wish for all of us to live together in the capital was in vain." Toyome was also in lower spirits than usual, but she assumed as stern a countenance as possible and remonstrated with him, saying: "How faint-hearted for one who wears a sword! Those redheaded bandits are not gods, after all, and you are not facing them alone. The God's oracle was a propitious one, and you will certainly return victorious. Don't say such inauspicious things!"

The bandits were only five in number, but each had the strength of ten men. They tormented their attackers mercilessly, but the soldiers outnumbered them. Two of the bandits were killed and another two were taken captive. The remaining one—the largest among them—pulled up a tree by its roots and brandished it about. No one was able to get near him.

Yoshinori was ordinarily weak-spirited, but the sight caused his warrior spirit to well up, and he cried: "Leave it to me. I'll bring him down!" He circled around to the rear and shot an arrow into the elbow of the bandit, who then could no longer hold up the tree. Yoshinori ran up and thrust his sword into the enraged bandit, who grabbed Yoshinori and tried to shove him over a precipice. Even while locked in the bandit's grip, Yoshinori never let go of his sword, and continued to gouge his opponent. The two of them, wrapped together in a deadly embrace, fell from the precipice. When the soldiers doubled back through ravines and reached the bottom, they found that the bandit's belly had been slashed open by the sword. Yoshinori's head had hit a rock at the bottom of the ravine. Each had died at the other's hand.

The governor praised Yoshinori and, along with the two captive red-haired bandits, presented a report of the valiant deed to the capital. For Yoshinori, the glory was posthumous.

Upon hearing the news, Toyome was prostrate with grief. Because of the words of a god who had possessed her body, she had senselessly lost her lover. Even if his welfare had not been at stake, she was struck by the presumptuousness of such an enterprise, whereby people's fortunes were set on courses for good or evil through the words of her mouth.

For these reasons, then, Toyome was loath to have her daughters become mediums. Only three years had passed, however, when the vengeful ghost of the third princess possessed Ayame's body and tormented Kaneie on his sickbed, though no one had ordered Ayame to act as medium. By then Toyome had already passed away and was thus spared the grief of seeing her daughter follow in her footsteps. Major Counselor Michinaga, who was concurrently serving as steward of the empress' household, asked Ayame to become a lady-in-waiting to his first wife, Rinshi. After what happened at Kaneie's sickbed, Michinaga had great expectations of the mediumistic powers Ayame had inherited from her mother.

A year later, upon hearing from Ayame that her younger sister Kureha had turned fifteen, Michinaga announced that he wanted to meet the young woman. He did not summon Kureha to his residence, but made a point of having her escorted to the hermitage of a nun who had served as his own nurse, and there he received the two sisters together.

Ayame had a slender build like that of her father and tended to keep her eyes cast down, but Kureha closely resembled her mother as a young woman, and had grown up to be very robust. Her complexion glowed like a peach blossom, and her smooth skin radiated youthful allure.

The elder sister's mediumistic powers had already been demonstrated. Kureha's hale and youthful appearance bespoke a nature completely different from that of Ayame, and Michinaga was somewhat disappointed. He nevertheless posed two or three casual questions, to which her answers were lucid, indicating a quickness of mind.

The sisters thought it a somewhat strange audience. Michinaga soon summoned Ayame and told her that for the time being he would maintain Kureha at the hermitage of the nun. He told Ayame to leave everything concerning her sister's future service up to him, and also strictly forbade her to tell anyone that Kureha was nearby.

Having thus taken care of matters, Michinaga one day paid a call at the palace of the empress. There he used the occasion to visit an old lover of his in the women's apartments, a lady-in-waiting named Shōshō no Kimi.

Shōshō had just finished helping wash the empress' hair. She had pulled out a screen and was lying down, but when she realized that Michinaga had come she hurriedly got up.

"Napping in the middle of the day! You're quite the proper young lady, aren't you?" said Michinaga jokingly as he sat down beside her, dispensing with formalities.

"Well, how sarcastic your lordship is! I just finished helping wash the empress' hair, and so I'm quite exhausted. Her hair, you know, is quite unlike anyone else's. It's utterly amazing that so much long hair could grow out of that little head."

"Really? It's such splendid hair, is it? . . . I'm sure it must be a lot of trouble to wash, then."

"It's really awful, I tell you. . . . Even with two or three of us working at it, it takes a long time before we're completely finished. . . . And then today, his majesty paid a visit in the middle of all that, and we were quite at a loss as to what to do."

To Michinaga, what Shōshō had mentioned innocently was more than of passing interest; these were all things that must be remembered.

"So, then, what did his majesty do? Did he wait patiently until you were finished washing the empress' hair?"

"No, he . . ." With a somewhat affected gesture, Shōshō put her cypress-ribbed fan to her mouth and smiled.

"He's still so young, and he just couldn't be patient. What's more, he insisted on seeing the empress today, so he had us bring a lot of old picture scrolls for him to look at while he passed the time."

His majesty, unable to wait any longer, finally just went right in after they had finished washing the empress' hair and were drying it.

It was summer, and the empress was sitting near a pillar in the main building where the blinds had been raised. She had three or four women fanning her newly washed, luxuriant black hair in order to dry it. Her skin, so white it looked as if it might melt like snow, was visible under the pale violet hue of her thin robe. That, combined with the luster of her hair spread out to cover her entire back, gave her an exotic mermaid-like beauty.

"Oh, your majesty... you mustn't come in here!" remonstrated an elderly lady-in-waiting. But the emperor appeared to pay no heed; he approached the empress and gently stroked her hair.

"Your hair is cold. I think I'll make it my bedding and go to sleep," he said in the tone of a spoiled child, snuggling his cheek against the empress' back. There was no way anyone could reprove the youthful emperor, but the ladies-in-waiting were worried lest the empress feel distressed. She turned, her countenance as serene as ever, and said: "If you make this your bedding, my coldness will penetrate you, and you'll end up as the frozen emperor."

With that she gathered the ends of her hair and pulled it up over the emperor with his cheek pressed against her, concealing his slight build behind a glossy, raven-black curtain.

The emperor laughed euphorically and remained motionless for a long time, buried in the empress' black hair.

Michinaga roared with openhearted laughter as he listened to Shōshō, but secretly he was astounded at the empress' talent for manipulating the juvenile emperor at will. Michinaga knew very well how deeply the tender affections of a beautiful, older woman can penetrate the heart of a youth, and he could not help being conscious of Empress Teishi as a future formidable rival if he should present his own eldest daughter in court.

After Shōshō finished her account of the incident, Michinaga mentioned casually that he would like to offer a junior lady-in-waiting to the empress' palace. It was a girl whose identity he could not disclose, and out of regard for the regent (his brother, Michitaka), he wished to avoid the public attention that would result from his making the offer himself. He asked Shōshō if she would not recommend Kureha's services, saying that she was the relative of an acquaintance.

Shōshō, unaware of Michinaga's real intentions, cheerfully took on the task and, assuming the knowing look of one who serves at court, said: "That will be easy. It just so happens that the empress' quarters now need one junior lady-in-waiting to serve as her majesty's personal attendant. I shall recommend this young woman's services, and say that she is my niece. What does she look like? Anyway, I suppose you're not saying anything about her family because she has your blood in her."

Michinaga thought it best to treat the matter lightly and go along with Shōshō's conjecture. "Well now . . . what can I say? I'll leave her in your hands. Just one thing, though—don't bring her up to imitate your amorous ways," he said as a parting remark, and roared with laughter.

Thus, without revealing her lineage and without any hindrances, Kureha came to serve at the side of Empress Teishi.

According to *A Tale of False Fortunes*, it was in the third year of Shōryaku (992) that Kureha of Miwa, assuming the name Kōben, came to serve as a personal attendant to Empress Teishi. The six years from the first year of Shōryaku—when Michitaka was appointed regent upon Kaneie's death—until Michitaka's own demise in the fourth month of Chōtoku 1 were a time of great prosperity for the regency, and it was as if Empress Teishi always had a brightly shining aura about her. It was during this time that Sei Shōnagon, author of *The Pillow Book*, came into Teishi's service.

The empress was then between her sixteenth year and her early twenties. In those days a woman was considered in her prime at that age, both mentally and physically. To the youthful emperor, who was just beginning to awaken sexually, the appeal of the intelligent and beautiful empress as an older wife was in every way complete, and through her an image of ideal womanhood took form in his heart.

Now the empress' mother, Kishi, had served as a court lady when she was young and was said to have composed Chinese poetry and prose before the emperor. Teishi inherited her mother's cultivation and was gifted with literary ability. Among aristocrats of that period, it was considered shameful for a woman to look a man directly in the face, and women who served at court were therefore thought somewhat immodest. It was truly an exceptional case for Michitaka, legitimate heir of the Fujiwara clan, to take as his first wife the daughter of a provincial official. Did Michitaka simply have an eccentric personality? Or was Kishi an unusually aggressive woman who cleverly led him on? At any rate, the personality of his own daughter, the empress, was somehow different from what was conventional for noblewomen of the period. Perhaps it was because of that difference that she was able so adroitly to rein a restive horse like Sei Shōnagon into a docile pony. In *The Pillow Book* is a passage—here paraphrased—denouncing men who took a trifling view of women serving at court:

> There are men who think that women in service at court are generally shallow, but this is a mistaken view. What is wrong with court service, after all? Such women are of course granted audience with the sovereign of the whole realm, and do not hide their faces in shame no matter whom they meet, be it a noble, a courtier, or an official of the fourth or fifth rank. If a man installs such a woman as his full wife, some will dislike her lack of reserve. On the other hand, even after her marriage she will be referred to as "Assistant Handmaid," and will be given access to court. She will be able to serve formally at the Kamo Festival, and will thus be a credit to her household. Moreover, if her daughters are chosen as dancers at the Gosechi Ceremonies, she will have the advantage of familiarity with the ways of the court and will not have to make hasty inquiries here and there.

Sei Shōnagon no doubt knew that the empress' mother had a background of court service, and this passage is possibly a calculated self-defense.

The author of *A Tale of Flowering Fortunes,* a lady-in-waiting to Michinaga's wife, does not write favorably of the regent's household. Even her use of such terms as "up-to-date," "in touch," or "disliking the abstruse" to describe the palace of Empress Teishi is actually a euphemistic criticism of the empress' lack of reserve and solemnity. It is hardly surprising, however, that the scintillating and witty atmosphere of Teishi's court should sway the youthful and still-maturing sovereign more than the old-fashioned, ceremonious refinement of his mother and her ladies-in-waiting. The empress' brothers, Korechika and Takaie, were always serving at the emperor's side, lecturing to him on the Chinese classics or teaching him to play the *koto* and flute. This also added to the brilliance and gaiety of her salon.

With the backing of the regent, Teishi enjoyed great material abundance as well. Kureha, a mere girl suddenly transplanted from rusticity to the brilliance of the palace, was at first bewildered by its splendor and sophistication. It was not long, however, until her young mind and body eagerly drank in the atmosphere. She concealed the incorrigible wild streak inherited from her mother and blossomed into a comely young lady-in-waiting.

Empress Teishi managed to give each of her ladies-in-waiting the impression of being the sole recipient of her special favor; in reality, though, she preferred cheerful and open dispositions. Compared to the citified, courtly, and excessively trim appearance of many serving in the palace, the innocence of Kureha's peach-like cheeks, the boldly cheerful expression of her eyes, and the lucidity of her words and manners had special appeal to Teishi, who came to have the girl serve at her side constantly. Whether at bath, at hairdressing, or even at night when she entered the bedchamber with the emperor, Teishi always had Kureha attending at her side, seeing to her every need. After three or four years, Kureha acquired a natural familiarity with the empress' facial features, the length of her hair, the shape of her hands, feet, and shoulders, her breasts, the transparent whiteness of her skin, and even the inflections of her beautiful voice.

There was more to Kureha's devoted service than just respect for the noble lady she served; the young girl had an almost erotic longing for the empress' graceful charm and uncommonly attractive features.

Kureha had at an early age been separated from her mother by death and was now unable to meet her sister, though she lived nearby. In a sense her fate was not unlike that of a prisoner, and yet she did not feel the least sorry for herself. She was supremely happy just to be able to serve at the empress' side, to perfume her gorgeous robes, and to massage her soft back and hips.

As steward of the empress' household, Michinaga occasionally went to the empress' palace to inquire after her welfare. Even if he saw Kureha on those occasions, he of course pretended not to know her, and even when he stayed with Shōshō, he made no particular inquiries about Kureha.

Shōshō herself generally broached the subject of Kureha during her bedtime talk. For about the first year, she praised the girl as a very perceptive junior lady-in-waiting, but after Kureha had obviously become the empress' favorite, Shōshō began to view her jealously as a rival female and no longer spoke well of her.

"At your lordship's request, I became a sort of 'room mother' to Kureha, but lately she has let the empress' favor go to her head and she pays no regard to the likes of me. Even when it's time to retire, she remains by her majesty's bedchamber, and doesn't come back to me." Shōshō spoke in a tone that presumed upon Michinaga's indulgence as she lay next to him, her head against the large sleeve of his robe.

"I wonder what it is about a countrified girl like that that appeals to her majesty."

Michinaga laughed broadly, then asked: "What about when the emperor visits? . . . Does she attend by the empress' side then, too?" As Michinaga spoke, he gently smoothed out Shōshō's disheveled hair, but his downcast eyes were coldly alert.

"I don't know what the empress is thinking in keeping an inexperienced girl like Kureha at her side even when his majesty visits. I have heard that his majesty's nurse has been spreading gossip that this is not proper. . . . If this were ever reported to the emperor's mother. . . . Even if she doesn't hear about it, there are already many in the emperor's household who criticize the empress' palace as too modish and as lacking in refinement, and they would not think well of it. . . ."

"I'm sure you don't have to worry about that. Even if someone were to tell the emperor's mother about it, I assure you that she would not make an issue of it. . . . But if Kureha is present to witness his majesty's intimacy with the empress, her own passions will no doubt be aroused. What a sinful thing." Even as Michinaga spoke, his mouth broke into a lewd smile and he lightly shook Shōshō's body in his embrace. "I have a request for you. How about it? . . . Will you ask Kureha what kind of intimacies are whispered between his majesty and the empress?"

"Well! Your lordship is perfectly awful!" Shōshō lifted her face from Michinaga's chest, her eyes brimming with coquetry. "His majesty is still young, after all. . . . Even if you heard, I'm sure there would be nothing of interest."

"But I want to hear all the more for that very reason. Just how does an empress treat a young emperor. . . ."

"Why do you ask? Your lordship must have learned that sort of thing a long time ago. . . ."

"No. I'm embarrassed to say so, but when I was a youth I never touched an older woman, so I have absolutely no experience that could give me a clue. Or, Shōshō, if you have ever taken a fancy to a nice-looking youth and initiated him to manhood, perhaps you could tell me about it."

"Well! What disgusting things you say! That sort of thing detracts from your character, you know. I grew up among many sisters, and I'm the first of us to have the kind of experience with a man that I'm having with you." Shōshō spoke in an affected tone, not really believing what she had just said. Again, she nestled up against Michinaga's chest.

When Michinaga visited Shōshō the next time, she was on leave at her parents' house. Her eyes glistened as she spoke: "I haven't felt well lately, so I've been on leave. The empress sent Kureha by with a sympathy gift of fruit and arrowroot. I thought I'd try to get out of her the information I had promised you, and gave her a long, narrow robe of pink color, the kind she especially likes. And then, I just casually asked about it."

"You went to a lot of trouble. But I suppose she was shy and didn't say anything."

"Oh, no, quite the contrary. She smiled and then proceeded to talk without a trace of reservation."

At this point, there is an abrupt shift of style in the account. Direct description of intimacy between the emperor and empress is avoided, and Kureha's narrative gives way to a discussion of the tender ages at which aristocrats married in those times, of circumstances under which men were seduced by older women, and so forth.

There is no doubt, however, that Michinaga was able to gain from all this a general knowledge of the imperial couple's sexual play. He was both excited and satisfied to ascertain even the one fact that the empress' voice—usually quiet and veiled, like flowing water hidden behind tall grass—changed in the bedchamber into an animated, ebullient voice, like the full-throated song of a bush warbler. *A Tale of False Fortunes* describes Michinaga's view of the empress in the following terms:

For all her seeming propriety and loftiness of purpose, she displayed a boundless capacity for treating someone in an endearing, charming, and coquettish manner. He thought it little wonder that those who served other noble ladies felt neglected by comparison.

Michinaga naturally wanted to know everything about the empress in order to raise his own eldest daughter, Shōshi, into a perfect candidate for imperial consort, and he used Kureha to obtain a detailed knowledge of as many of Teishi's daily routines as possible.

Once or twice a year Kureha visited the old nun who had been Michinaga's nurse. After reverently leading the girl before the Buddha and having her worship, the old woman always admonished her: "You must never forget that it is through his lordship's kindness that you are in service to the empress. He wishes to make the empress his model for the upbringing of his own eldest daughter. You don't have to say anything now, but when his lordship has need for you to speak, you are to tell him all you know."

Kureha always felt strangely oppressed when she was with the old nun, but would respectfully promise before parting, "I shall do as you say."

She did feel it somehow underhanded that her having entered the empress' service through Michinaga's connections was kept secret from everyone, but young Kureha had absolutely no way of guessing what lay at the bottom of his scheme. Thus between ages fifteen and eighteen she remained in the service of Empress Teishi, in a world of splendor and opulence.

We read also in *The Pillow Book* that Regent Michitaka, on the twenty-first day of the second month of Shōryaku 5 (994), ordered a memorial service to offer a complete set of sutras to the Sakuzen Temple at Hōkōin. The empress was present at that event, and Kureha was in attendance behind her, dressed in a five-layered, long-sleeved robe. That was no doubt the grandest day in the young woman's life. And yet, though the splendor of the regent's household seemed then like a blossom whose petals would never scatter, the services at the Sakuzen Temple were to be its last evening glow. After that, cruel blasts of wind would be the beginning of a long winter.

Chapter Two ⟋

Emperor Ichijō's mother, Senshi, was Michitaka's and Michinaga's sister by the same mother. She was known as the Higashisanjō Empress, and later, after taking the tonsure, as the empress dowager. It was through her influence that her father Kaneie became head of the Fujiwara clan and had the way open to hold sway over the entire country as regent; thus neither of her brothers would be outdone by the other in carefully attending to her wishes. From her childhood, however, Senshi had had a particular fondness for the youngest, Michinaga, believing that he possessed talents superior to those of his elder brothers. She secretly hoped, therefore, that Michinaga might be an advisor to her own son, Emperor Ichijō, but she was only too well aware through the history of her own ancestors that, blood relationships notwithstanding, struggles for political power could give rise to vicious feuds. For that reason, she was careful to betray no partiality toward Michinaga now that Michitaka had assumed the regency.

There was no doubt in Michitaka's mind that his political position was Senshi's sole stay of support, but in reality she harbored a constant and deepening anxiety of which only her youngest brother Michinaga was actually aware.

The emperor was of course her dearest son, but he had been at a tender age when he was elevated from crown prince to the throne, and the empress dowager could not help feeling that, as he increasingly assumed a public persona, the loyal affection he ought to have had for his mother alone was being diluted by his love for the new empress.

Empress Teishi was a niece to the empress dowager. According to the customs of that time, there was nothing exceptional about a wife's being older than her husband, and if Teishi were a submissive young woman who had simply been raised in a somewhat liberal manner, the empress dowager would certainly not have grown so anxious. And yet, as an aristocrat's daughter who had been brought up with the utmost care, Teishi was endowed with scintillating talent, and the fact that the emperor appeared to find this very refreshing invited his mother's jealousy.

In fact, as mentioned previously, a fashionably new salon was beginning to take shape around the emperor under the influence of such talented young nobles as Korechika and Takaie, with their sister Teishi as a binding force. That so peculiar a lady-in-waiting as Sei Shōnagon was able without restraint to display her brilliant talent to the astonishment of the courtiers actually owed to the bright and free atmosphere that had grown up around Teishi. And, to the extent that the young emperor's tastes were cultivated as a member of that salon, the empress dowager was saddened by the thought that he was gradually becoming estranged from her.

The empress dowager hinted at those feelings in oblique terms to Michitaka, who, being a good-natured sort and fond of drink, did not listen sympathetically, but rather made a joke of her pensiveness and evaded discussion of the matter.

It was in the fourth month of Chōtoku 1 (995)—the year after the services at Sakuzen Temple—that Michitaka passed away. From the first month, he had lost his appetite and would drink only water, and thus had grown quite gaunt. Within two or three months there was little hope for his condition. From spring of that year an epidemic spread in the capital; countless people died every day, and there were not a few well-known nobles and courtiers who succumbed to this malady.

However, that was not Michitaka's illness. In all likelihood, his digestive system was damaged by alcohol poisoning. By the third month, he himself no longer seemed confident that his illness could be easily cured and, upon secretly seeking an audience with the emperor, petitioned that during his illness his eldest son, Palace Minister Korechika, be appointed as acting regent.

The emperor was sixteen years old at the time and had developed sufficient discretion in matters to render a decision. He thus approved the petition, and on the eighth day of the third month a proclamation was issued to Korechika that during the regent's illness he should "execute government over the entire realm and all officials therein." Senshi, the Higashisanjō empress dowager, was of all people both surprised and displeased to hear news of the proclamation.

Through her feminine intuition, the empress dowager sensed that someone was pulling strings behind the scenes for the emperor to have made an immediate decision on such an important governmental affair without consulting her, his mother. That "someone" was Empress Teishi, who, the empress dowager was convinced, had bent the emperor's heart to herself using the caressing and servile looks of an elder sister, and who was tearing the emperor away from his mother.

The empress dowager, who at that time was in Ichijō's palace, was in attendance at court one day and invited the emperor to a room in the Kokiden Palace. He entered wearing a white informal court robe with a twilled floral design, the openings of the freshly scented sleeves loosely pulled back to show a crimson undergarment. He had grown taller during the brief time she had not seen him. His boyish innocence was gone, and though he was her child, he seemed to the empress dowager very dignified and somewhat constrained in her presence.

The emperor, too, looked nostalgically on his mother's beauty as he beheld her in her nun's guise, a crimson garment visible under her black robe, her ample black hair cut shoulder-length and spread out like a fan.

"In the short time I haven't seen you, you've become quite a man, and have grown very handsome. . . ." The empress dowager looked fixedly at the emperor's appearance, and held the sleeve of her nun's robe up to her eyes. "At any rate, the regent's illness is really too bad, isn't it? I hear that he has grown quite thin."

"Yes, he called at the palace one evening at the beginning of the month. Though he is by nature genial and joking, now he has become thin as a shadow. Even his voice sounds somehow withered. It's so depressing that I couldn't help crying."

"It makes me think of my father. My older brother is still only about forty. I would never have imagined that he would fall victim to such a terrible illness. The empress must be very worried, I suppose."

"Yesterday she returned home to visit him. Among all of his children, the regent was especially fond of the empress and the palace minister, and so her grief seems to be all the greater."

"That's no doubt the case. . . ." The empress dowager bowed her head ostentatiously. "Be that as it may, there is a matter about which I should like to caution you. Will you listen?"

"Of course, whatever you say. . . ." Even as he spoke, it occurred to him that his mother's advice would no doubt be about Korechika, as usual. Even when Michitaka had come to him under cover of night, the emperor had said he would like to discuss the matter with his mother, but Michitaka would not give in.

"If you discuss this with the empress dowager, she will certainly advise you to have either Michikane or Michinaga act as regent. I don't say this merely out of flesh and blood attachment; it is precisely because Korechika is young that he has the temperament to take the reins of government. Moreover, your majesty has attained manhood now, and the empress will no doubt give cause for celebration before long. But even if she gives birth to your first son, if either Michikane or Michinaga is in power at the time, that prince will have absolutely no hope of succeeding to the throne. If your majesty's love for the empress is truly deep, I beg you to give heed to my request. . . ." Michitaka had been in tears as he presented his petition, his frail body withered and bent like a leafless tree. Considering that the emperor had for some time been fond of the young Korechika's comely appearance and his superior gift for learning and music, and that, moreover, the empress had the utmost confidence in her brother, the emperor could not very well reject the petition of the seriously ill man before him.

Nevertheless, when the empress dowager put it to him so tenderly, he could not help feeling guilty for not having sought her opinion in advance. The glow of the lamp against his face, with his habitually downcast eyes, had a feminine beauty about it. When the empress dowager sensed his contrition, she thought it too cruel to scold him openly. Drawing upon the precepts of the retired emperor En'yū, who had passed away some years ago, she delivered a detailed lecture on governing, stressing the importance of maintaining a clear distinction between public and private, and reminding the emperor that those who are young and inexperienced must revere the opinions of their elders. She concluded in an unusually stern tone: "In this case, since Korechika's appointment is only for the duration of the regent's illness, I shall not say anything. This is not an agreeable thing to talk about, but if worse comes to worse for the regent, the one who succeeds him would also be responsible for determining and ordering the course of your reign. When that happens, I shall very much resent it if you fail to discuss the matter with me." To the empress dowager, Korechika and the empress were also blood relations: nephew and niece. Based on the degree of intimacy, though, she had set her sights on Michikane and Michinaga—especially on her youngest brother Michinaga—and after Michitaka's death, she would not be pleased to see political power passed on to Michitaka's talented posterity. She was beset with anxiety at the possible outcome if Empress Teishi should join forces with her elder brother, Korechika. It was upon Teishi that the youthful emperor bestowed all of his special affection. Though her mother, Kishi, was the upstart daughter of a provincial official, the other ladies-in-waiting and imperial concubines faded in obscurity before Teishi like stars before the moon.

Empress Teishi had grown up under favorable circumstances and was gifted with both intelligence and beauty. She was unable to harbor the secret machinations others imagined, and one might conclude it was because she in no way felt inferior to them. Thus if she seemed downcast by her father's illness, she was in low spirits for that reason alone, and resorted to no such strategies as making a tearful and clinging entreaty to the emperor in an attempt to keep political power within her father's household. The very guilelessness of her own heart prevented the empress from realizing that she was watched with such guarded caution by the empress dowager, for whom she felt only compliant respect as the emperor's mother and as the most noble lady of the Fujiwara clan.

One might say the situation of the defenseless empress was that of being caught between parties struggling for power, people who were keeping a vigilant and unceasing watch on her. Many of those who knew Teishi well enough to recognize her exterior beauty and sparkling wit knew nothing of the purity of her heart, which was as limpid as fresh water. Because of her all too dazzling beauty, the empress was easily misread as having a demonic ability to manipulate the emperor. In her naive innocence—her inability even to conceive of such scheming—lay the seeds of the adverse circumstances of her later years.

Upon perusing the annals of history, whether of the East or of the West, one finds any number of heroines who followed a hapless course of fate leading from a seat of glory to the bottomless depths of misfortune. Such women as Marie Antoinette, empress at the time of the French Revolution, and Kenreimon'in, whose life was woven into the sad history of the fall of the Taira clan, were main characters in such tragedies, and it would seem the sorrow experienced by Empress Teishi in her declining years—except for the fact that it was not stained by any sanguinary incidents—hardly pales in magnitude compared to these others.

On the tenth day of the fourth month of Chōtoku 1, Regent Michitaka passed away at the relatively young age of forty-three. It was only natural that Korechika, who earlier had been commissioned by the emperor to act in Michitaka's stead as regent during the latter's illness, should desire to maintain a grip on the reins of power and succeed to the position of regent, just as his father had wished. For his young age, Korechika excelled in learning and ability and was, moreover, of a handsome appearance. In others' eyes, he thus was a flashy figure, but this only served to fuel the antipathy of many of his seniors at court who had been displeased for some time with Michitaka's partiality in promoting Korechika—barely in his twenties—to the position of minister ahead of the latter's uncle, Michinaga.

The opinion of those people was as follows: "The regency is an important position, controlling the government of the realm. While the emperor is young, major appointments of trusted advisors are of utmost importance, and an unseasoned, unreliable youth posing as a man is not up to the task. We will not stand for the government's being played with as if it were a child's toy." The chief proponents of this view undoubtedly included the Higashisanjō empress dowager and her brothers Michikane and Michinaga. Moreover, this opinion was supported by many courtiers driven by an intense clannishness that objected to the progeny of Kishi—not a Fujiwara—wielding authority at court.

At this time the bereaved Korechika had no recourse but to rely on Teishi's ability to captivate the young emperor's heart. Korechika explained their family's common interests to Teishi, who had returned home prior to her father's death, and anxiously petitioned her support. Teishi herself no doubt wanted her beloved elder brother to be appointed to the regency. With these things in mind, she returned to the palace on the twelfth day of the fourth month in spite of the ritual pollution of her father's death. She was not permitted to meet with the emperor for the duration of her pollution, so she took up residence in the Tōkaden Palace, some distance from the Seiryōden Palace. *A Tale of False Fortunes* records the matter in roughly the following manner.

After the dusty Tōkaden Palace was hurriedly swept and cleaned, the empress arrived. It was a departure from precedent to return to court before her father's funeral services were completed, but both the palace minister (Korechika) and her grandfather Takashina no Naritada earnestly maintained that there was no other way but to try to win over the emperor at this time. Thus she resolved to return. The steward of the empress' household (Michinaga) soon heard of her plans and gave her notice—pretending that it was by order of the empress dowager—that since it would be improper for anyone polluted by death to meet with his majesty, she should refrain from seeing him.

"That's our uncle, shrewdly staking out his position as usual!" guffawed the empress' younger brother, Middle Counselor Takaie, seemingly amused by his own remark. Then he added nonchalantly, "There's nothing to be concerned about. Compose a letter and have it delivered to his majesty secretly. He'll be sure to take the initiative of coming to you tonight." The middle counselor was still only seventeen years of age and did not possess the gracefully handsome features of his elder brother. His imposing countenance, with its long, drawn-up eyes, looked very much like that of Michinaga as a young courtier. His disposition also was openhearted, and Michinaga secretly liked the fact that this young man showed no diffidence to those who were self-conceited. Of all the sons of his elder brother—with whom he had not been on good terms—it was only toward Takaie that Michinaga was friendly. He often invited this nephew to accompany him on hunting expeditions, or to drink together.

Although Takaie pressed the empress to write a letter, she hesitated to do so. Before she had the chance to take up the brush, Ukon no Naishi, the lady-in-waiting in attendance to the emperor, visited the Tōkaden Palace after dark.

The empress was in mourning, and was wearing a dark gray outer garment, yet she stood out among the young ladies-in-waiting clustered about her, all of whom were wearing the same robes of mourning. The empress' grief-stricken appearance, with her sleeves drawn together, was so captivating as to surprise an observer that, depending on the wearer, dark robes could arouse such wistfulness.

"Since he has not seen your highness' face for some time now, I can tell that the emperor is not in good spirits. With due respect for your highness' grief, I ask that you take strength and meet with him. . . ." Ukon no Naishi's tone was encouraging as she handed the emperor's letter to the empress, who wiped her eyelids, swollen from weeping, and opened it. Looking at the beautiful, masculine cursive hand, the empress could not help feeling pleased that in the short time she had not seen him, his handwriting had matured to such neatness. Although he was the first man with whom she had been intimate, in the mind of the empress—who was five years his senior—he was always like a younger brother on whom she lavished affection.

Michinaga had already told the emperor that he must not meet with the empress because she was mourning the regent's passing. Yet knowing that she was within the same palace compound, he simply had to spend at least one night with her. Since she could not be openly summoned, would she mind mingling with the ladies-in-waiting who would be returning with Ukon no Naishi? He missed her sorely, and moreover there were many things he needed to discuss with her. . . .

Such was the gist of the emperor's letter. For some time the empress buried her face in the letter, her comely eyebrows beneath the forelocks tumbling over her face alternately appearing and disappearing as her eyes followed the vertical cursive lines. Although she was older than the emperor and possessed an unusually intelligent nature, her status in society was nevertheless backed by few years, and she had, up to that point, not been tempered by adversities. Fortune had been on her side when she, as the regent's daughter, had met with favor. Now, with the sudden passing of her father, even Ukon was pained by thoughts of the fate that might be looming before the lovely empress.

Thus the empress ended up going secretly to the emperor's evening quarters, mingled in the ranks of Ukon's attendants. There is no way of knowing what kind of sweet nothings passed between the two royal personages that night, but the emperor seemed to accept the empress' petition, and was of a mind to have Korechika continue in the regency.

Although the ladies-in-waiting attending the emperor were strictly forbidden to tell anyone about the empress' secret visit, it was immediately made known to the steward of the empress' household. Michinaga at once informed the empress dowager, who went to Teishi the next day and determined that the latter's residence would henceforth be the upper quarters of the Kokiden Palace, which was linked to the emperor's evening quarters by a single passageway. The empress dowager would easily be able to maintain surveillance, and it would henceforth be impossible for the empress to visit the emperor in secret. In spite of their proximity, it was as though they were separated by a raging torrent. They were reduced to helpless fretting, with no way to speak to one another.

In deciding whether formally to appoint Korechika to the regency or to hand it over to Lord Awata (Michikane), who had already been made minister of the right, the emperor had interests at stake that were in every way equal to those of the empress dowager, of Korechika, or of Michinaga. For that very reason Michitaka had given the emperor a warning shortly before his death. The empress dowager summoned the emperor to her quarters and once again admonished him, saying that appointing Michikane to the regency would be an impartial and magnanimous decision, the kind of judgment a sovereign should make. The emperor was astute enough to grasp the reasonableness of what his mother was saying, yet his heart was heavy when he recalled the promise he had made to the empress.

"The minister of the right has been afflicted lately by the illness that is going around, and doesn't seem to be in good health. Even if I appoint him to the regency, would he be able to hold up to the demands of such a position?" The emperor raised his downcast eyes and spoke with hesitation, to which the empress dowager responded with a spirited laugh, "The minister of the right isn't yet thirty-five. Even if he is ill now, I can't imagine that he would suffer the same misfortune as my older brother. But then, if by chance something untoward should happen, you could cross that bridge when you come to it. Considering the future of the regency, I can't imagine that anyone will accuse you of an inappropriate action. If you appoint Korechika to the regency at this time, neither Michikane nor Michinaga will think well of you for it, and I am certain that disorder would follow."

"I realize that too, but..." The emperor looked at his mother with a nonplussed expression while he nervously stroked his knee with one hand. Then he said, his cheeks flushed, "Mother, I'm thinking of what might happen if the empress were to conceive in the near future."

"That, too, is something to consider if and when it happens. If the empress should bear a male heir, then the regency would of course be handed over to Korechika." The empress dowager's tone was magnanimous, but secretly it occurred to her that the possibility of the empress' giving birth to a prince was all the more reason to hold Korechika's advancement in check now; otherwise, she would face irreversible setbacks.

The empress dowager was not very fond of Michikane, but she always allied herself with him and Michinaga in opposing the former regent's household, and in this case Michinaga also wanted the reins of power to be entrusted to Michikane. "If that should happen, it is all the more fitting at this time that the regency should be entrusted to Michikane," said the empress dowager calmly. "Even if the empress does conceive sooner or later, we don't know whether or not the child will be a prince. But if it is, he will certainly be crown prince. By the time the prince is officially installed as prince imperial, you'll be at the prime of manhood. And by that time, if Korechika has prepared himself and is in public service, he, too, will make a wonderful trusted counselor. Up to now, Korechika has been shown excessive favor by his father, the regent, and has come to think that he should always have his way about things. There is something arrogant about his attitude. If he were to attain the regency in that state of mind, he would end up becoming conceited, and might even slight you. When my late father was young, he, too, was out of favor with his older brother and for a long time bemoaned his fate. When he later took the reins of government, though, he was all the more attentive to everyone both above and below him, and was praised as an outstanding head of the Fujiwaras. Each human being is endowed with his own fate, and it isn't necessary to go to extremes to take advantage of the circumstances of the moment. If one really has the capabilities, one's time will certainly come around."

The empress dowager's words conveyed the calm reassurance of her many years' experience; they had about them a compelling strength that the young emperor was powerless to resist.

In the end, he yielded to his mother's persuasiveness and on the second day of the fifth month issued a proclamation appointing as regent the minister of the right, Michikane, who was recuperating from an illness at the home of one Sukeyuki, former governor of Izumo.

The empress was at that time still in the Tōkaden Palace. She was perceptive enough to anticipate that the reins of power would likely be handed over to Michikane according to the empress dowager's entreaty, and even when she saw her ladies-in-waiting in a state of distraction, weeping with disappointment, she did not lose her composure.

Middle Counselor Takaie was the first to visit her, and said: "You're weak after all, aren't you? At this rate, you'll never win in any future rounds with the empress dowager."

In spite of her younger brother's reproachful tone of voice, the empress said with a faint smile, "You still don't understand the mind of a woman. No matter how spineless I seem to myself, when I really consider the matter, it's the emperor who is to be pitied for having to agonize over this. I can't bear to look at him. If I said this to our older brother or to our grandfather, there's no telling how much they might resent me for it. But yesterday when I heard that it had been decided to appoint Michikane to the regency, I was actually relieved."

"It's disheartening to see that you're so weak-spirited, you who ought to provide the focus for our family now that our father has passed away. But the recent proclamation on the regency is only a formality at this point, and both Korechika and I think that the real battle is yet to be fought. Michikane is ill from the current epidemic, and is only getting worse. His life will probably soon end. What is really frightening is not Michikane, but the next person."

"You mean the steward, Michinaga?"

"That's right. I've been on rather close terms with that uncle of ours, but in my judgment, if the power of government passes on to him, I'm afraid it will never return to our family. The empress dowager looks on him with special favor, and I think she secretly harbors a desire to have the regency given to Michinaga rather than Michikane." Upon saying this, Takaie drew closer to the empress and tugged at the sleeve of her dark gray robe. "If such a time comes, then you must not fail to manipulate the emperor's feelings. No doubt, it must be painful for him to think that he has disappointed you and Korechika this time. And, of course, his majesty misses your affection. But think, too, of what will become of the prince who is sure to be born eventually. Korechika is very talented, but there is something weak-spirited about him, and as a politician he is no match for our uncle. But I'll be able to help our brother. I may be young and of low rank now, but one day when the prince you'll bear grows up, I'll be his advisor and wield as much power as our uncle. At certain times, of course, political power shifts because of circumstances, but at the same time it's also a showdown. As far as I can see, the sway you hold over the emperor is in no way weaker than that of the empress dowager. What is weak is your own spirit. Resolve that you will not give in if another opportunity like this should come around. Otherwise, you're sure to regret it later."

Takaie's words were spoken softly, but his eyes were brimming with an intense light.

The empress heaved a sigh and said, "I don't believe that sort of strength of character is in me. All of you are unfortunate to have such a spineless sister."

"You speak that way, but the rumor among everyone on the side of the empress dowager and our uncle is that the influence you have on the emperor's mind is just like that of Yang Kuei-fei in China."

"The fact that they see me as Yang Kuei-fei has less to do with me than with the Japanese and Chinese books I studied under our mother's guidance since I was small. People may talk about a woman's talents, but it seems to be difficult for them to ascertain her personal character. In my own real intentions, there is no such bold cunning at all."

As the empress spoke, there was in her noble visage an unusual, severe luminance, like that of the moon on a cold night. For a while Takaie stared at her silently, as if absorbed by his sister's austere mien, but then he reminded her, "At any rate, the hopes of our entire family are hanging on your resourcefulness. I shall not mention this again. Please, give this matter serious thought. . . ." Then his demeanor brightened, and, after giving instructions with a self-assured, male air on such things as the arrangement of the decorations in the hall, he took his leave.

After Takaie's withdrawal, the empress sat lost in thought for a time. She then wrote a letter in elegant, cursive hand on light gray Chinese paper and summoned Kureha. "You are to give this letter to Ukon no Naishi, saying that it is a reply from Shōnagon. There will no doubt be people like the emperor's old nurse keeping an eye on him for the empress dowager, so be careful not to attract their attention. Please, be sure to give it directly to Ukon."

Kureha nodded attentively at the empress' instructions as if to show that she had comprehended each one of them. Ever since the late regent had become ill, the empress had been weighed down by many worries, and Kureha was moved to pity to see that her mistress' round white cheeks looked as if a layer had been whittled away from them. It occurred to her that the empress had not met with his majesty for a long time. Kureha herself was attuned to such subtle emotions because she had recently come to know love herself. Her lover was not one of the courtiers in service at the empress' palace who joked with the ladies-in-waiting, and so the affair did not come to anyone's attention there. She was in love with the secretary of the imperial police, a young military officer named Tachibana no Yukikuni. The women serving at court cared only for the aristocracy, and showed no regard for such as the imperial police, who had the ignoble occupation of handling criminals. Kureha disregarded that and was alone in having such a lover. Her affair with him had begun with a dramatic episode: on returning from her usual secret visit at the New Year to the cottage of the nun who had been Michinaga's nurse, Kureha's party was attacked near Sagano by bandits. Her attendants fled, and as she was about to be kidnapped, she was rescued by Yukikuni who, as luck would have it, was passing by. Following the description of this episode, *A Tale of False Fortunes* notes:

However, this too had something about it that bespoke Michinaga's cunning. Yukikuni was a handsome young man with a strong constitution, and Michinaga often gave him charge of tasks, saying that he was the surest among the Imperial Police to accomplish an assignment. By having someone save Kureha at a critical moment on her return from the nun's cottage and thereby turning her maidenly feelings toward her rescuer, Michinaga had prepared an underling to perform an important service. Afterward, putting two and two together, it could be seen that everything was thoroughly arranged according to Michinaga's wishes.

Michinaga had probably seen that Kureha's adoration of the empress verged on homosexuality, and he therefore furnished the young woman with a suitable man as a lover before her passion for the empress could turn into dedication. Both Yukikuni and Kureha played into Michinaga's hands, neither having any knowledge whatsoever of his intentions. Korechika, of course, was unaware of all this, and even Takaie, the most astute in the late regent's household, had no knowledge of these circumstances.

When Kureha took the empress' letter—purportedly to Ukon no Naishi from Sei Shōnagon—and presented herself at the evening quarters where his majesty was staying, she was not surprised when it appeared the empress dowager was also there. Ukon no Naishi hurriedly gave Kureha a meaningful glance and called her to come by the side door, where Kureha announced: "I am told that this is a reply from Shōnagon in the form of Japanese verses based on Po Chü-i's Chinese poems that were recited the other day." Thereupon, Ukon made an appropriate nod and said, "The empress dowager is here this evening and we are very busy. Please tell Shōnagon that I'll write a reply early tomorrow morning."

Upon opening it after Kureha had left, Ukon saw that it was not from Sei Shōnagon, but rather a letter from the empress addressed to the emperor. She set it down next to the emperor, who had already retired to his bedchamber, and, still worried that she might be overheard, whispered, "Please look at this when no one is around. Be sure not to leave it lying about. . . ." The emperor also realized what it was and, giving a nod, slipped it nonchalantly into the breast of his robe. After ordering his valet to bring the lamp closer, he opened the letter with feelings of nostalgic anticipation, cautiously shifting his eyes to both sides of the bedchamber, as if he were entering the path of secret love.

He was immediately touched by the beautiful, feminine cursive hand written in a confusion of dark and light shades. The gist of the letter was as follows: When I came to you in secret at night, I begged you to appoint my brother Korechika as regent, but I learned yesterday that my wish was not granted. However, I do not consider your majesty to be heartless. Rather, by making such a request, I have put you in a difficult position between myself and the empress dowager, and I am saddened to imagine how painful it must be for you. Because the empress dowager is also in the upper quarters—and because I am tainted by the pollution of my father's death—I cannot very well come to your side for the time being, but henceforward please do not concern yourself about me. Make the decisions you judge in your heart to be right. The longer I am away from your majesty, the stronger are my feelings of yearning for you, eclipsing even my grief for my late father.

It appeared that the empress had been weeping while writing. Just to see that the handwriting appeared to be blotted here and there by tears brought vivid memories to the emperor's mind, as if she were right beside him: the feel of her black hair, glossy as if cold and wet; the softness of her white skin, which seemed as if it might vanish along with him if he embraced it. A maddening longing for her permeated his body. The more he thought that she must be suppressing her feelings out of consideration for him—in spite of appearances and the usual cheerful and ebullient wit of her words—he could not help regretting that he had appointed Michikane to the regency.

However, just as Takaie had predicted, it was but briefly that the family of Michikane—who had been stricken by an illness then rampant—would be delirious with joy at his appointment to the regency. At the hour of the ram (2:00 P.M.) on the eighth day of the fifth month, after only seven days, he expired like a bursting bubble. He was thirty-five years old.

Thus the only remaining opponent with whom Korechika had to contend for the eagerly sought-after regency was his uncle, Michinaga, who was eight years his senior. As far as both the emperor and the empress dowager were concerned, if Michikane had remained healthy and continued in the position, there ought to have been no need for another sharp exchange of opinions between parent and child, but when misfortune is added to untimeliness, the matter cannot simply be left alone.

In relating the events that followed, *A Tale of False Fortunes* follows the text of *A Tale of Flowering Fortunes* and simply records:

> *On the eleventh day of the fifth month, a proclamation entitled "The Realm and the Service of Government Officials" was issued naming the Major Captain of the Left (Michinaga) as Regent, making him quite without equals. Since it voiced the Empress Dowager's long-cherished hope, she was deeply gratified.*

However, as is attested by the record in *The Great Mirror,* both the empress dowager and Michinaga himself appear to have spared no efforts in securing this proclamation to the regency, and in all probability, this account was closer to the truth.

The emperor was reluctant to have Michinaga take the reins of power as regent. He felt sorry for the empress, who was already without backing after the death of her father, and he could imagine how galling it must be to her to see power passed to her youngest uncle, Michinaga, with whom she was not on good terms in spite of their blood relationship. Even in Michikane's case, the emperor had not felt certain about the decision for those same reasons. The empress dowager did not think well of Korechika, and dismissed the emperor's opinion, saying, "What would happen if you entrust the government of the realm to a mere boy like that? Doesn't even the children's song say, 'If you want melons, first go get a container'?" She spared no words in her attempt to dissuade him: "Really, my late brother indulged Korechika too much. How painful it must have been for Michinaga, who is his uncle and many times more talented, to see his nephew promoted to palace minister ahead of him. Well, you were young then, and had left everything up to the late regent, so it really couldn't be helped, but it would be too heartless of you this time, after having once entrusted the regency to Michikane, not to give it to Michinaga. Of course, neither Michinaga nor I would be pleased, but beyond that, anyone versed in court practices would be sure to think it improper."

The emperor was taken aback by the earnestness visible in his mother's countenance, and sensed in it an even more determined opposition than she had put up on behalf of Michikane. And yet, there was a tightness in the emperor's breast every time he thought of the unfortunate empress, and he avoided giving a definite answer. Whenever he was with the empress dowager, he was always being taken to task about something. Finally it became annoying, and he stopped going to the upper quarters where she had her residence.

The day on which the appointment was to be made, Michinaga, too, was so worried that he came to the Kokiden Palace to ask the empress dowager how the talks with the emperor were going.

Beneath her black robe, the empress dowager was wearing Chinese yellow figured cloth, and her locks, trimmed but still somewhat long, waved to and fro on her shoulders in maidenly fashion. Her noble bearing, long looked upon as representing her clan's prosperity, still shone like the full moon in her youthful visage, which today seemed more dazzling than ever.

"His majesty doesn't like to meet with me, and has been evading me. Today, I think I shall go to the evening palace and stay there all night if I have to until he is convinced. Please don't go back, just wait here. . . ." Having said that to Michinaga, who was leaning his wooden scepter against the veranda, the empress dowager quietly disappeared out the door. She felt tense with desire to see how much power she, the emperor's mother, had over his feelings.

With that, the door to the passageway connecting the Kokiden Palace and the Seiryōden Palace was shut tight, and for over two hours not so much as the sound of a cough escaped from the room where mother and son had met. The hour for the evening roll call of the courtiers was long past. Though it was a summer night, dew was falling on the veranda, and occasionally the faint yellow glow of fireflies flitting about in the garden would skim by Michinaga's sleeve or court cap as he crouched down there.

Did the fact that no imperial sanction was forthcoming for a long time mean that the emperor would not accept what the empress dowager had to say? If that was the case, he would need to go ahead with his second plan to beat the empress and Korechika. Such were Michinaga's thoughts as he sat there cross-legged.

Close to midnight, the door opened suddenly and with vigor, as if it had been forced open from within. The figure of the empress dowager as she emerged, the hem of her pleated skirt illuminated by the paper candle her attendant was holding, appeared before Michinaga's eyes like a vision of a bodhisattva. Though her face was red from weeping and glisteningly moist, the corners of her mouth lifted into a cheerful smile as she said, "Finally, the proclamation has been issued." Michinaga gulped involuntarily, crawled up to her on his knees and, lacking the composure to utter a single word, buried his head in the hem of her robe and wept. She, too, seeing how her usually intrepid younger brother was deeply moved, pressed her face into her sleeve.

Thus the position of regent was given to Michinaga, empowering him both to lead the Fujiwara clan as its chief and to issue commands to the entire realm.

Compared to the power of Michinaga, which grew more resplendent, like the morning sun, the fortunes of the nobles of the late regent's household were irretrievably on the decline, like the sunset.

The only thing Korechika and Takaie were able to rely on was the emperor's affection for the empress, but even that had been unable to stand in the way of the empress dowager's insistence that Michinaga be appointed to the regency. Just as in the song "Change your tactic and the sky becomes cloudy, overturn it and it rains," those in society who keenly followed shifts of power eschewed as imprudent an alliance with Korechika's household or any seeking of his favor.

At times like these, the natural thing for a veteran of such contests to do would be to endure patiently and wait for an opportunity for a comeback. As nobles who had become thoroughly accustomed to having fortune on their side and who took favorable appointments for granted, however, neither Korechika nor Takaie made any attempt to flow with the current of the times; rather, they tried to maintain their wounded dignity by putting up resistance. In so doing, they played into Michinaga's scheme to bury them, and ended up seeing their graves being dug before their very eyes.

Some events in *The Tale of Genji* are thought to have been modeled on the fates of people living at that time. After the death of the Kiritsubo emperor, the rival forces of the family of his elder brother's mother, Kokiden, held a monopoly on influence at court, leaving Prince Genji in an isolated and helpless position. Genji failed to remain circumspect and was not careful to avoid those things that would invite censure. Instead, he deliberately rekindled an old love affair with the emperor's favorite daughter, Oborozukiyo, having one tryst after another with her until it resulted in his being stripped of his office and forced into self-imposed exile in Suma. In that section, Genji's dissoluteness—which, in spite of his fear of the strength of those in power, led him to behavior mocking that power—suggests inner plays of emotion similar to those of the brothers Korechika and Takaie who, not a year after power had shifted to Michinaga, were stripped of their offices and banished to distant Kyushu and Izumo. They were charged with assaulting retired emperor Kazan in a disturbance that, likewise, grew up around a favored imperial daughter.

It was a year after Michinaga had assumed the regency, in the fourth month of Chōtoku 2 (996), that this measure was enforced, and it was also at that time that Empress Teishi first conceived and was carrying the emperor's child. As far as Michinaga was concerned, the fact that the emperor's favorite consort was pregnant with the first imperial child rather necessitated the permanent ousting of his close relatives Korechika and Takaie from positions of power.

Chapter Three ～

After Michinaga had assumed the regency and taken the reins of government, two new ladies-in-waiting were installed to attend the emperor. One was Genshi, the daughter of Akimitsu, the Horikawa minister of the right, and the other was Gishi, the daughter of Major Counselor Kinsue. Genshi was called Lady Hirohata and had her residence in the Shōkyōden Palace, while Gishi was quartered in the Kokiden Palace. Both were from reputable families and had aspired to court service, but as long as the former regent was in power they held back, fearing that they would be eclipsed by the empress' influence, which was at its zenith. Now that power had shifted to Michinaga, who personally encouraged them, they resolved to present themselves at court.

Now Michinaga did in fact have a daughter of his own, but she was still at the age when girls run and skip, and he could not very well have had her installed at court. Under such circumstances, then, the greatest obstacle he faced was the ability of the empress to captivate the emperor with her charms, and it became necessary for the new regent to use someone—it did not matter whom—as a wedge between the two. Through various connections, Michinaga was able to learn a great deal about the features and dispositions of the two new ladies-in-waiting. Genshi was the granddaughter of Kanemichi (who had always been on bad terms with his elder brother, Kaneie) and, as might therefore be expected, had been raised in an old-fashioned manner with an emphasis on refinement and decorum in all things, but she lacked an engaging charm. Gishi was attractive enough, to be sure, but was not very adept at music and was somewhat dull-witted. Neither possessed a temperament to match that of the empress, and Michinaga could plainly see that, by the time his own eldest daughter would come of age, neither would be a serious rival for the emperor's favors. He was therefore able, with peace of mind, to encourage their installment at court. It would be to his advantage, too, if his majesty should become somewhat infatuated with the new ladies-in-waiting and if princes were born to them. Michinaga was confident of his own power to shift the position of such princes about in any manner. The only unsettling prospect remaining was that of a prince born to Teishi.

However, Michinaga's plan to dampen the affections shared by the emperor and empress was not successful. The emperor did enter into perfunctory intimacies with the ladies-in-waiting living in the Shōkōden and Kokiden Palaces, but such dalliances merely made him realize anew that, as a woman, Teishi was quite without peer in beauty, gentleness, and intelligence.

After Michinaga had succeeded to the regency, the empress returned for a time to her parents' home. Messengers came several times each day bearing letters from the emperor. The ladies-in-waiting and others in the emperor's retinue began to exchange glances, tugging at one another's sleeves and gossiping about how his majesty suddenly had so much to say.

The empress, who had returned to her parents' home in the fifth month, again entered court on the nineteenth day of the sixth month and was quartered in the Umetsubo Pavilion. After her return, the emperor rarely went to the quarters of the new ladies-in-waiting. It was a blissful picture of special favor, not unlike that described in the verse from the "Song of Everlasting Sorrow": "Of the three thousand beauties at court / His love for the one equaled that of three thousand."

The empress dowager was then making frequent trips between the court and her parental home, and at the same time secretly keeping an eye on the relationship between the emperor and empress. That autumn, when she was at the Ichijō Palace, her head felt heavy and her shoulders and lower back began to ache. After taking to her bed, she would occasionally be plagued by fits of coughing and labored breathing. Both the emperor and Michinaga were extremely worried, thinking that it must be some kind of evil spell or that she must be possessed by a malevolent spirit. They summoned the abbot of Hieizan, called in all other priests renowned for miraculous spiritual powers, and had them spare no effort in offering prayers of protection.

Courtiers and warriors close to Michinaga occasionally warned him, "This is no doubt the work of Palace Minister Korechika. He is resentful that the regency was given to your lordship and has the impertinence to have a curse placed on the empress dowager. As a matter of fact, they say that the minister's maternal grandfather, Naritada, is practicing all manner of spells, boasting that he will place a curse on your lordship, too, to bring about your demise just as he did with Michikane. If we don't do something soon, then not only the empress dowager's life, but also your lordship's, might be placed in jeopardy." Of course, Michinaga was not unaware that the holy man was performing elaborate rites, but he did not for a moment think his own life would come to an end through such misdirected maledictions. Michinaga's long-held ambition had been realized: he had become the head of the Fujiwara clan, and as he seized power over the entire realm, he beamed with confidence. Michinaga had been aware for some time that the abilities of the quick-witted Korechika, his junior in years, were in reality somewhat superficial, but now that he occupied the premier position of government, he was able to look down upon Korechika and the entire household of the former regent from an exalted vantage. Korechika was no one to fear. The disquieting ones were Empress Teishi and the former regent's second son, Takaie, who was said to be an unruly sort. If a first prince were born to the empress—and if Takaie gave this prince his full backing, both publicly and privately—then Takaie would enjoy the complete trust of the emperor, and his political influence might be welcome both in the capital and in the country, as if he himself were regent.

Considering these circumstances, it occurred to Michinaga that, in order to shore up his own position, isolating the empress from the emperor was of greater expediency than moving Korechika out of the way.

A Tale of False Fortunes reports the condition of the empress dowager's illness in the following manner:

> *The Regent watched apprehensively as it became apparent that her condition was deteriorating day by day. Moreover, her frequent fits of coughing and her plaintive weeping seemed to come from beyond waking consciousness. Concluding that it must be the work of an evil spirit, his lordship gathered priests renowned for their efficacious prayers and had them perform, without interruption, the rituals to the Five Wisdom Kings.*
>
> *His Majesty, too, was so troubled by his mother's condition that he was unable to do anything. She had turned thirty-six that same year, but was still young in appearance; her figure was at its prime, and it seemed a shame that she should be a nun. He continually lamented his father's untimely demise, and now if the Empress Dowager should pass away as well, then he felt he would be unable to continue his own reign. One day, he went in secret to the Ichijō Palace.*

When the emperor's visit was announced, his mother was so pleased by his filial sentiments that she had her pillow raised, her disheveled hair combed, and her appearance freshened. When the emperor was brought to the empress dowager, he was both encouraged and gratified to see that her complexion looked better than he had expected. Of course, Michinaga was at her side.

The empress dowager had been suppressing the spasms of her illness, but at length she was again overcome by them and pleaded, pain in her voice, "Please leave.... I do not wish to have you see me lose my dignity." She bent down, leaning over on an armrest. Michinaga said, "This happens all the time, and the pain seems to be getting steadily worse." He then signaled the priests to resume their prayers, which they had stopped while the emperor was present.

Among the ladies-in-waiting caring for the empress dowager was one who suddenly began to shake as if she had been doused with cold water. In an instant she bent her body like a bow and began to writhe, and then stood up and went toward the emperor.

Michinaga was startled and, restraining her with his wooden scepter against her skirt, sharply rebuked her: "Look here! Where do you think you are? Don't you know you're in the presence of the sovereign of the land? What kind of fox deity has possessed you to commit such an outrage?" Michinaga's air was all the more imposing because he was ordinarily indulgent and calm. On this occasion, his mien was such that even gods and demons would likely shrink from it. Nevertheless, the young lady-in-waiting, dressed in a scarlet skirt with a blue outer garment, seemed to have no fear of the regent's authority. She smiled and said, "That's not for you to say, uncle. I am dearer to his majesty even than his own mother. He always says that rather than part with me, he would give up the throne. What, then, is wrong with my going to his side?" Then, managing her graceful train, she lightly straightened the skirt Michinaga had been restraining, and smoothly drew up to the emperor.

"Your Majesty, have you forgotten me? Just last night, when you came to the Kiritsubo Pavilion, didn't you recite 'The grasses of love/Piled up high in seven carts/In seven great carts . . .'?*" It was an unusual spectacle to see the lady-in-waiting place her hand on the emperor's knee and gaze at him with gentle reproach. It was nevertheless exactly like the empress' solicitous and consoling manner, and left the emperor dumbfounded.

---

*From a poem by Princess Hirokawa in the Man'yōshū:

Koigusa o	The grasses of love
Chikaraguruma ni	Piled up high in seven carts,
Nanakuruma	In seven great carts—
Tsumite kouraku	This surfeit of love
Waga kokoro kara.	Comes from my heart.
IV:694	

This young lady-in-waiting was none other than Ayame of Miwa, who barely a month before had come to serve in the palace of the empress dowager.

His majesty had never actually witnessed a spirit possession, much less by a spirit appearing to be the "living ghost" of his beloved empress, who seemed to be cursing his mother. He so lost his composure that he was covered with gooseflesh and was a pathetic sight: hopelessly transfixed, the color draining from his face, and perspiration oozing around the edges of his hair as he bit his colorless lips.

"Your majesty is unaware that the empress dowager is envious of your affection for me. That is why you did not grant the regency to Palace Minister Korechika, and that is also why you do not intend to give the throne to the prince who is now in my womb. Because your majesty's filial devotion is deep, you will not contravene what your mother says. As long as the empress dowager remains alive, not a single ray of light will dispel the gloom of my life. Even as your mother curses me, so do I curse her. No one knows about the imprecations now being performed by my grandfather, but when those rites are consummated, the empress dowager's life will vanish like morning dew. This shall be your mother's recompense for her having despised me."

With that, Ayame of Miwa buried her face in her sleeve and laughed in an uncanny voice. To his majesty's ears it was none other than the coquettish laugh of the empress when she tried to stifle all sound from escaping their bedchamber. Though the wan, twitching face bore no resemblance whatsoever, he could not help feeling that the empress herself was lying prostrate before him. At that very moment the empress dowager began to tear at her own breast and bent herself backward as if someone were strangling her. The emperor cried out, "Mother, mother!" and, shoving the armrest out of his way, tried to go to her side. Michinaga caught him by the sleeve. "You mustn't go near her. The high priest will see to it that the malignant spirit is exorcised from that crazed medium of a lady-in-waiting. The empress dowager will shortly feel better. Your majesty must not come in

contact with any evil influence. I beg you to leave immediately."
Practically wrapping the emperor in the sleeve of his own garment, Michinaga also withdrew from the room. Surrounded by screens in a room to the side of the main hall was the hellish scene of the exorcist, his face painted vermilion, intoning mystical formulas in a high voice and whipping the lady-in-waiting with his rosary, her hair dishevelled and utterly wretched to behold.

Even after returning to the imperial palace that night, the emperor did not go to the Umetsubo Pavilion. He was torn between feeling guilty for having broken his promise to the empress and a perennial desire to bury his cheek in her cold black hair and worship her smooth, sleek skin until his heart was set ablaze. At the same time, he was chilled by the all-too-plain maliciousness of the maledictory words pronounced by the medium at the Ichijō Palace.

The emperor was well enough able to imagine that the empress, who had not succeeded in her backing of Korechika for the regency, might not bear amiable feelings toward the empress dowager, but when he had been alone with his consort, she had never once spoken in a derogatory manner about his mother. Even when the regency had been given to Michikane immediately after Michitaka's death, the empress had sent a letter to the emperor from the Tōkaden Palace showing a gentle, sisterly solicitude at a time when he was caught between pleasing her or his mother.

"Such a malicious curse couldn't possibly have come from her heart. I wonder if it might not be a plot by those in my mother's camp to drive us apart."

After returning to his palace that night, various thoughts passed through the youthful emperor's mind about the wretched medium he had seen that day. His love for his consort was so deep that at length he found himself speculating on the motives of that lady-in-waiting. But then, how could he account for the fact that the demeanor and speech of the medium were identical to those of the empress? Particularly, how could anyone but Teishi herself have known of the verses "The grasses of love/Piled up high in seven carts / in seven great carts," which he had recited in the bedchamber just the night before? Such thoughts gave him an uneasy feeling that perhaps some sinful, feminine karma was lodged in the empress' heart and was manifesting itself through such uncanny workings.

Of course, the emperor did not mention this incident to anyone. To the personal attendants and ladies-in-waiting, though, who were serving that day in the Ichijō Palace, it was shocking to see the empress' living ghost attacking the empress dowager, and they could not very well keep it to themselves. Among the valets who never left the emperor's side was the lover of a lady-in-waiting in the Umetsubo Pavilion, and he recounted to her what happened at the Ichijō Palace that night when the emperor did not go to the empress. Amazed and alarmed, the next morning the lady-in-waiting relayed the story in a hushed voice to Chūshō, the empress' nurse.

Chūshō had thought it strange when the emperor did not show up the night before, and she nodded understandingly. She did not have the courage to inform the empress of such a matter right away, however, but waited for an opportune moment to call Ukon no Naishi, who had come to deliver a letter from the emperor to a paneled door somewhat removed from the empress' presence, and there inquired about what had happened the previous day. Naishi's face betrayed a degree of consternation, and, fumbling with her cypress-ribbed fan, she said, "The gossip has spread rather quickly, hasn't it? Only the empress dowager, his majesty, and the regent were present at the scene, so I can't claim to have witnessed it myself. The countenance of one of the young ladies-in-waiting serving the empress dowager changed suddenly. She was no doubt possessed by an evil spirit, but the claim that it was the empress' living ghost is just the babbling of vulgar types who are fond of spreading stories. His majesty has said nothing about it."

Ukon no Naishi, in the usual manner of those experienced in service at court, tried to put the matter in a harmless and inoffensive light. When further prevailed upon by Chūshō, she could no longer conceal it and ended up telling what had happened on the previous day, couching her account in vague terms. Actually, Ukon, too, had plainly seen through a bamboo blind the dreadful mien of Ayame possessed by the spirit of the empress, appearing noble and at the same time alluring.

"That's impossible! I know her highness' thoughts very well. She is not the kind of person who could ever do so shameless a thing as curse or despise someone. If she were really so strong-minded, she would have done everything in her power to prevent his majesty from appointing the minister of the left to be regent, and things would not have turned out this way. The palace minister and the middle counselor are chagrined that she didn't try harder. But as you well know, the empress has slept with his majesty ever since he was just a boy and has taken care of him as if he were a younger brother. Because of that, his majesty has been all the more attached to the empress. Their love is a beautiful thing that has nothing to do with matters of government. To say that she turned into a living ghost and placed a curse on the empress dowager. . . . It's just too awful. . . ." Nurse Chūshō, overcome by emotion, broke off in the middle of her sentence and sobbed, pressing her face into her sleeve. Ukon no Naishi herself was well acquainted with the empress' usual cool temperament and, even having seen the spectacle of the medium the previous day, did not want to believe it was true. But the sight of Ayame possessed by an evil spirit had simply been too vivid, and Ukon could not rule out the possibility that even in so refined a person as the empress there lay hidden, like a coiled serpent, vindictive feelings as can only be found in a woman's heart.

Within a day or two the rumor had spread like fire through the women's quarters surrounding the emperor's palace, each messenger speaking in hushed tones with knitted brows and nervously batting eyes.

Korechika was surprised to hear the news from the senior assistant minister and hurried to the palace, but when he saw the calmly smiling face of the empress, who was unaware of the matter, he was unable to say anything about it and, after making some conversation on social matters, left her presence. He could not imagine that she, of all people, could harbor such malicious resentment. On the other hand, he accepted the reality of spirit possession and could not dismiss as groundless the possibility that the rancor and chagrin they felt at the adverse political situation should possess the empress also, or even that such subliminal enmity should eventually be directed against the life of the empress dowager. Takashina no Naritada, the grandfather of Korechika and the empress, was, in fact, continually performing secret prayers prohibited outside the court in order to place a curse on the empress dowager and Michinaga. Now that the empress' pregnancy had been confirmed, there was a strong possibility that the regency could return to her clan should anything happen to the empress dowager and Michinaga.

It never occurred to Korechika that the emperor's heart might move away from the empress because of this incident. On the contrary, it seemed to him that, since the emperor had until now always presumed upon the empress' tenderness, there might rather grow in him a sense of awe that would cause him to take his consort more seriously. It is, certainly, typical of a person whose fortunes are declining to entertain only a hopeful view of matters and to indulge in wishful thinking, but Korechika was far more optimistic than Takaie in his estimation of human nature.

It was Takaie who candidly reported the matter to the empress. Unlike his elder brother, Takaie gave absolutely no credence to the news that his sister's living ghost had menaced the empress dowager. As he spoke, the empress' face—usually radiant as crystal water on a clear day—was overcast with shadows of fear and sadness. Her right arm quivered as she drew an armrest close to her, creating faint waves at the sleeve opening of her many-layered garment. After hearing him out, she sighed heavily. "Our older brother, Chūshō, and Ukon no Naishi all know of this, and yet they didn't say anything to me, did they? Everyone is secretly thinking that maybe I really am cursing the empress dowager, aren't they? It's never apparent, after all, what is in people's hearts. And besides, given the empress dowager's low estimation of me, well, I myself could not say that I adore her either."

As she spoke, the empress flipped back the hair hanging over her cheeks as if annoyed by it. It was a slight gesture, but clearly the usual gracefulness of the empress was weakened, and it was pitiful to Takaie to see that she had been hurt so deeply by this.

"You're the only one who believes me, aren't you? You surely understand that I'm not such a vindictive woman that I would turn into a living ghost. You'll go see his majesty and tell him that, won't you? I think the reason he did not come to see me last night or the night before was because the dreadful evil spirit he saw at the Ichijō Palace gave him a fright. I feel sorry for his majesty that he is troubled by all this. Tell him to come to me tonight no matter what. If only he can see my face, then the troublesome suspicions will melt like ice before the morning sun. . . . "

Watching the unusually animated keenness of the empress' eyes and the movement of her lips on her flushed face, Takaie believed that if the emperor really met with her, his suspicions would easily be dispelled.

"I'm not worried about his majesty's feelings. It's just that, through this event, it's plain to see that our uncle is anxious to dampen the emperor's passions for you. Most likely, the lady-in-waiting who was the medium picked up your mannerisms and way of speaking from someone who is familiar with your daily deportment. You were just being imitated. Times being what they are, you must be careful about the kind of people serving at your side. Sei Shōnagon, especially, has her eyes on you. From the time he was steward of the empress' household, our uncle took delight in Shōnagon's wit and was always making conversation with her. What's more, they say Shōshō no Kimi has become very withdrawn lately, but people know she is one of the regent's lovers. Both Shōnagon and Shōshō are clever women, and it doesn't seem likely that either would do something reckless. But, just as a master may be bitten by his dog if he is not careful, you cannot be too certain about what those two might do. I plan to say this to his majesty as well, but you must be cautious, too."

After stressing this point to the empress, Takaie went to see the emperor. His majesty seemed somehow pensive and dispirited. Takaie attributed it to the fact that it was a day of abstinence, and proceeded with an animated account of a hunting trip to Ōharano two or three days earlier. Only after that did he mention that the matter of the empress' living ghost appearing in the palace seemed some kind of fraud.

The emperor himself was approaching such a conclusion after reflecting on the matter from various angles and having considered the empress' usual behavior. He thus felt relieved when he listened to Takaie, as if a burden were being lifted from his shoulders. At the same time, he felt all the more ashamed that he had doubted even for a moment the purity of the empress' heart.

From that evening on, the emperor once again began to frequent the empress' quarters. Just as she had predicted, when they met face-to-face and talked intimately, holding one another's hands, and when he felt her skin and become entangled in her black hair, all suspicion of her vanished like a dream.

Fortunately, the evil spirit did not reappear and the empress dowager improved somewhat. After a month had passed she returned to full health, and the dark rumors that had spread about the empress also faded away for a time.

In the meantime, there were other episodes: of Sei Shōnagon's being so chagrined at the failure of her collusion with Michinaga that for a while she did not appear for service; and of Shōshō no Kimi's returning to her parents' home on the pretext of illness. During this time, however, Kureha continued her dutiful service as before at the empress' side, unsuspected by anyone. She had grown so tall and her body had so filled out that the empress remarked laughingly to the emperor: "Kureha has suddenly grown tall, hasn't she? When I was inside the main building and saw her walking on the other side of the bamboo blinds, I mistook her for one of those tall boys who attend you."

Although no one took note of her reaction, when Kureha heard about the crazed behavior of the empress' living ghost at the palace of the empress dowager, a fear stabbed her and for a while she was dumbfounded. It was all too plain to her that the medium had been her elder sister, Ayame, to whom she herself had described the details of the empress' voice, choice of words, and every aspect of her deportment.

Michinaga was a farsighted schemer, and in using the two sisters as false mediums, he had employed as intermediary Kureha's lover, the secretary of the imperial police, Tachibana no Yukikuni, rather than go directly through his nurse, the elderly nun. It had no doubt been painful for both Ayame and Kureha not being able to contact one another for two or three years, though they were both in court service in the same city. Yukikuni, who from time to time had heard Kureha express longing for her sister, called for Ayame to come to his house once when he had brought Kureha there, and thus arranged for the two sisters to meet secretly. The text of *A Tale of False Fortunes* relates the particulars of this meeting as follows.

> *Yukikuni arranged for the two sisters to meet, whereupon their regret at years of not having been allowed to see one another vanished instantly. They set aside all formalities, weeping and laughing as they talked. Kureha presumed upon the affection of the elder sister whom she had not seen for a long time, looking up at her from her yet-juvenile face. When they had finished talking about various things, including their late mother and their home-town of Nara, Ayame said that his lordship (Michinaga) had heard from Shōshō no Kimi that the empress' appearance was without equal, and that in order to educate his eldest daughter as a candidate for imperial consort, he was anxious to have her study the features and manners of the empress. Shōshō no Kimi mentioned that whenever he met with her, he hinted at his pleasure in hearing all of the smallest details of the empress' appearance and behavior. Yukikuni, who was sitting to the side of the two sisters, commented, "That's rendering good service to your lord. Nobles with daughters aspiring to become imperial consorts don't have a moment's rest." Kureha didn't have the slightest doubt about her older sister's intentions, and*

after that, every time they had occasion to meet, she taught her to imitate the empress' mannerisms and voice. Yukikuni himself had no idea that it was a plot on the part of Michinaga. For Ayame, it was difficult to refuse her lord's command to play the part of a medium at the appointed time, and she undertook the assignment. Since his majesty was to visit the empress dowager on the morrow, Ayame wrote a letter asking if there had been no old poems exchanged among last night's intimate bed talk to which others would not be privy. Kureha, thinking nothing of it, had written back telling of the poem on "The grasses of love." Later, when she recalled it and put two and two together, she realized she had been duped, that her elder sister had become a false medium and had shamelessly used the imitations she had learned from her to play the part of the empress' living ghost before his majesty. Fear seized Kureha's heart. She felt as if she had caught a terrifying glimpse of the bottom of the regent's heart, like a murky abyss where a great serpent lived. When it occurred to her that his having been their guardian these several years, looking after their every need, was only part of a plot to create a rift between the empress and his majesty, she realized they had made vain her dead mother's earnest entreaty to Kaneie that he not use her two daughters as mediums, that she had seen with her own eyes the evil that could come of it and had learned a bitter lesson from it. Her sorrow was boundless as she thought that now her sister, and even she herself, had been turned into pathetic false mediums.

Kureha's conscience was further seared to see that even after that, the empress did not appear to harbor the slightest suspicion of her. She even thought of quitting court service but soon abandoned the idea, realizing that if she left the empress' side another intermediary would simply take her place. Rather than allow that to happen, she resolved instead to protect the empress from that point on, whereby she could atone for her sin of unintentional betrayal and perhaps even merit a little of the empress' benevolence. Kureha was somewhat relieved to hear later that Yukikuni had not taken part in Michinaga's nefarious plot. After that, she received a letter from Ayame filled with apologies and excuses, but she felt no inclination ever to meet her sister again.

Notwithstanding the fact that she had grown up under Michinaga's protection, before she knew it she found herself in the thick of a political battle. She was entangled by the cords of power and interests and was being made to dance according to them, and she felt wretched in the extreme.

Chapter Four ⌁

On the twenty-fourth day of the fourth month of Chōtoku 2 (996), an imperial edict was issued banishing Palace Minister Korechika to Tsukushi [Kyushu] and Middle Counselor Takaie to Izumo. One year after the death of Michitaka, it was obvious the sun had set on the declining fortunes of the former regent's household. The barrier that had existed between Michinaga and Korechika was related to the rivalry between the empress dowager and the empress for the affections of the emperor, and all parties concerned realized that the barrier was growing wider by the day. Impressed indelibly in the empress dowager's heart was the vivid image of the empress' cursings delivered by Ayame of Miwa on the day of the imperial visit. Of course, she would have thought it vulgar to speak of such things to his majesty or to Michinaga, but when she heard that Korechika was having rites of imprecation performed against her, she appeared convinced that all of the former regent's household, beginning with the empress, were hoping for her demise.

The two brothers were like drowning men, sinking to ever greater depths. Both Korechika and Takaie (who was supposed to have been the most intelligent in the family) were given over to the arrogance peculiar to youth from prospering and influential families accustomed to the world's favor, and they lacked the prudence to acquiesce, which would have protected them in times of adversity. The main charge resulting in their banishment was the incident on the sixteenth day of the first month of that year when Takaie, together with his retainer, shot an arrow at retired Emperor Kazan, who was stealthily returning from a tryst with his favorite mistress. Thus Takaie himself furnished an excellent excuse to the forces loyal to Michinaga.

Kazan, the son of Emperor Reizei, was the elder brother of

Danjō no Miya (Prince Tametaka) and Sochi no Miya (Prince Atsumichi), both of whom later gained notoriety for their affairs with Izumi Shikibu. Both of the younger princes had been born to the imperial consort later known as Grand Empress Chōshi and thus were the grandsons of Higashisanjō Kaneie, but Kazan himself was the son of Kaishi, daughter of Chancellor Koretada, so his blood ties to the Higashisanjō family were not strong. Like Reizei, he seemed to have a mental disorder and was often given to eccentric behavior. Kaneie therefore soon had him abdicate and tried to have the throne given to the first prince born to Emperor En'yū and his own daughter, Senshi. It is well known how Kaneie's second son, Michikane, sought to carry out his father's wishes by tricking the emperor, having him secretly slip out of the palace and go to Kazan-ji Temple to have his head shaved. Though Michikane promised that he would follow the emperor in taking the tonsure, at the last moment he broke his promise and stole back to his home. It was rumored that Michikane's sudden death as he was doing obeisance before the regent was some kind of retribution for the sin of having deceived the emperor.

It was that sort of unforeseen incident that had caused him to step down abruptly from the throne, but he nevertheless referred to himself as a "monk retired emperor" and, with no apparent qualms about what the world might think, lived in a grand style, occupying himself with sporting matches, hunting, and chasing women. Even the Higashisanjō household, aware, at the time of his abdication, that the world knew of their unjustifiable treachery, made no effort to curb the priestly former emperor's self-indulgent ways.

Takaie's motive for almost shooting retired Emperor Kazan with an arrow was not the satisfaction of his own feelings; rather, his action was fueled by the jealousy of Korechika, who at that time was paying visits to the daughter of the Ichijō regent (Tamemitsu), and who had heard that Kazan likewise was in love with her and was calling on her secretly. Actually, the object of Korechika's passion was San no Kimi, and it was her younger sister, Shi no Kimi, whom Kazan had been wooing, but Korechika misunderstood, thinking that his own lover had been stolen away, and consulted with Takaie to see if there might not be some means to keep the retired emperor away from her. Takaie, who ordinarily took pains to keep his natural unruly boldness in check, was tantalized. "Fine, I'll take care of that. Just leave it up to me!" Takaie seemed amused by Kazan's excitable temperament and once before had wagered with him: it was agreed that Takaie would, together with fifty or sixty retainers, rush into the retired emperor's gate in ox carts and that the retired emperor would lead his own retainers against them. However, Takaie had been unable to break through his opponent's defenses and ended up returning, thereby losing the wager. At the time he admitted defeat, saying, "I was no match for his royal aura of authority." And yet there was something about the incident reminiscent of two naughty boys with a friendly rivalry. Partly for the fun of it, Takaie volunteered to shadow retired Emperor Kazan, lie in wait for his return, and scare him. In *A Tale of Flowering Fortunes,* this passage is narrated as follows.

Perhaps Takaie planned to frighten the Retired Emperor, who was returning on horseback one bright moonlit night from the Takatsukasa Mansion. At any rate Takaie shot an arrow through the Retired Emperor's sleeve. Now to be sure, the Retired Emperor was a very brave man, but this was an extreme situation, and it was only natural that he should have been frightened. He was terrified and returned to his palace quite distraught. He ought to have reported this incident at court and to the Regent (Michinaga), but the circumstances under which it occurred were of course awkward. He was embarrassed and determined not to tell anyone, not wanting it to be a shame to posterity. However, the news spread at court and reached the Regent's ears. The details were out in the open, and there was no longer any hiding it; it became the chief item of gossip.

Far from thinking this a troublesome incident, Michinaga seized upon it as a good opportunity to turn opinion against the two brothers. At any rate, the disquieting rumors—that they had placed a curse on the life of the empress dowager, or that

Korechika had commissioned the Daigen Service, a rite properly limited to the court—had all been eclipsed by their one distinct act of attacking retired Emperor Kazan. All at once, the gathering rain clouds had turned into a terrific thunderstorm, pelting down upon the household of the former regent.

As soon as Korechika, who had been depending on Empress Teishi as the clan's mainstay of support, saw that misfortune was beginning to multiply around him, he invited the empress to his Nijō residence and put her up in the main hall. Her mother, Kishi, and her grandfather, Takashina no Naritada, among others, perhaps held the view that leaving her at court, where Michinaga's power was most evident, would bring some unforeseen misfortune upon the pregnant empress, who went to her brother's residence incognito and under cover of night. Out of diffidence to Michinaga, few attended her, but Kureha never left her side as she went to Korechika's Nijō residence. While Kureha was dutifully seeing to all of the empress' needs, that fateful day arrived: the twenty-fourth day of the fourth month.

On that day, powerful military commanders—Korenobu, former governor of Mutsu Province, Koretoki, lieutenant of the Left Gate Guards, and Yorimitsu, former governor of Bizen—rode into the palace compound at the head of their troops and set up innumerable encampments. The crown prince's guards and the main palace guards stepped up a rigorous watch over comings and goings through the gates and prepared for an emergency. The ostentatiousness of Korechika's arrest, in spite of his obvious lack of military force, was calculated to demonstrate the regent's power. It was also a scheme to sever, once and for all, the bonds of the emperor's affection for the empress —bonds that tied him to the former regent's household.

It was common then for yin-yang divination masters to say that natural disasters portended armed disturbances, and in this case, too, various rumors were noised about. Respectable aristocratic families made defensive preparations, and even insignificant merchant families prepared to flee with their belongings on their backs in case of an emergency. Everyone seemed stricken with panic.

In the former regent's household, it was the younger Takaie who alone was managing everything with a cheerful countenance in the midst of all this. He realized that Michinaga's exaggerated posturing was aimed at consigning his family to oblivion, and that behind it lay a formidable hostility toward the empress and himself. Yet he wore a complacent smile in spite of such private bitterness.

Had Korechika been a bit bolder in his judgment, Takaie would have been quite prepared at any moment to invoke the afterglow of his late father's glory and have a showdown with Michinaga. In light of his brother's surprising faintheartedness in these trying circumstances—and of the empress' pregnancy —it occurred to him that this time there was simply nothing for it but to lie low and plan a later comeback.

A number of soldiers and court officials had for years taken up residence with Korechika and served him as retainers, but when they saw that the household was decidedly in decline, they became anxious about their own welfare rather than their master's safety. They pilfered household belongings, some even making off quietly with metal fixtures. Thus human nature, ever duplicitous, only further disheartened members of the family.

From the early evening of the twenty-fourth, all of the imperial police in the capital were gathered at Nijō, tightly surrounding Korechika's residence on all sides. It was a frightening scene to behold as they crowded about, their swords and halberds drawn and at their sides, leaving no space even for an ant to escape.

All the key figures in this incident, including the empress, apparently were gathered in the main building of the compound, yet a dead silence reigned within. Since there seemed to be no one about, the soldiers entered as far as the garden and the connecting corridors and peeked inside. Just catching glimpses through the bamboo blinds of the rough-looking men, their armor glistening, was enough to terrify the women and children inside, who began wailing.

Kureha's lover, Tachibana no Yukikuni, was of course included in this group of imperial police. He recalled that Kureha utterly despised her elder sister Ayame for her role in playing the part of a false medium. Moreover, Yukikuni knew that Kureha harbored suspicions of and resentment toward himself. Realizing that her devotion to the empress had only grown more unshakable since that incident, he imagined how utterly mortified she would be if she knew he was playing a part in this massive arrest. He loved Kureha's undefiled passion of mind, and the prospect of enduring her contempt because of this was indeed painful. But it was of course impossible for one in the service of the court to refuse an imperial command.

At about the hour of the serpent (10:00 A.M.), the encirclement parted for an envoy of imperial messengers, imposingly clad in red robes and bearing swords and scepters, who ascended the stairs to the balustrade of the main building and went inside.

Korechika had, together with his mother and other family members, clustered about the empress within the curtained dais in the main wing, but he could not remain indefinitely in tearful dejection. Prodded by Takaie, he went out into the side room to confront the imperial messengers, who embodied the will of Michinaga. Seemingly quite unmoved by Korechika's appearance, one of them read the imperial edict with a completely dispassionate air in clear, sonorous tones. The charges therein were as follows: the crime of having cursed his majesty, the retired emperor (the monk retired Emperor Kazan); the crime of having a malediction pronounced upon the mother of the emperor; and the crime of secretly sponsoring clandestine performances of the Daigen Service, which was prohibited to anyone outside the court. As a result of committing these three crimes, both Palace Minister Korechika and Middle Counselor Takaie were banished and demoted to governor-general of Tsukushi [Kyushu] and provisional governor of Izumo, respectively. Such was the gist of the edict. As the messenger was reading it, the sound of weeping women, accompanied by the rustling of silk, surged like waves from within the bamboo blinds of the main wing. The crying of the residence guards added to the rising volume until the entire main building seemed to swell with grief. Korechika himself was pressing his face into his sleeve and, sobbing like a bullied child, seemed unable even to answer.

Takaie, who alone amid the mounting lamentation was not crying, fixed his usual strong gaze on the messenger and answered: "We have duly received the words of the edict. It will be necessary to make preparations, and we ask for a period of indulgence until we can depart." The messenger, guessing that the empress was in the room, descended the stairs with the same expressionless look and without making a more forceful pronouncement, but he summoned one of the chamberlains in attendance, Secretary of the Imperial Police Yukikuni, and commanded him, "You are to see both the governor-general and the provisional governor off to their respective places of exile today. It is the lord regent's command that they leave without delay." With that, the messenger departed.

Yukikuni was distressed that this command should have been given to him of all people—and at such an inopportune time—but he could do nothing about it. He was worried lest some of the country warriors who had been sent in for special reinforcement and who were ignorant of propriety might try to storm the building, and summoned to the balustrade the elderly Norimasa, former governor of Hitachi and one of the remaining loyal stewards of the former regent's household. "At this point, there would be no way for you to resist. It would be a different matter if it were only we imperial police, but the place is swarming with warriors from all over the country. They are ignorant of decorum, and if they should force their way in, it would amount to lèse-majesté toward the empress. I shall try somehow or other to arrange for a slight delay in your departure. Please tell the middle counselor that they should be on their way by dawn tomorrow."

Norimasa nodded several times, his face pressed to his sleeve, as he listened to Yukikuni's offer. Then he went inside. At length he came out and requested in an almost sobbing voice, "Both her highness and the palace minister say that they are pleased with your kindness in this matter. At any rate, they will need until tomorrow morning before they can depart. We ask that the imperial police see to it in the meantime that no ill-mannered men force their way inside."

Yukikuni discussed the matter with his superintendent and

others among the police and reported to the palace that they would wait this one night.

That day, Michinaga remained in constant attendance at the Seiryōden Palace, never letting the emperor out of sight, ostensibly to protect his majesty. In reality, however, he was maintaining careful surveillance lest in his absence a proclamation of pardon for Korechika's and Takaie's offenses should result from the emperor's affection for the empress, thereby undoing all Michinaga had planned for so long and so carefully. The empress dowager had also come to the upper quarters in the Kokiden Palace and was likewise keeping an eye on the emperor.

In a radical departure from his usual magnanimity, on that day Michinaga assumed a severe attitude toward all court officials, seemingly unwilling to overlook so much as a hair out of place.

When the report came from Nijō that Korechika's and Takaie's departure would be delayed, Michinaga straightened his scepter and commanded sternly: "An imperial edict is not to be negotiated according to personal sympathies. Properly speaking, those two ought to have been tied to their carts and sent off. See to it that they leave the capital tonight! Anyone who takes an imperial edict lightly, whether the imperial police or soldiers of the Taira or Minamoto clans, will be held accountable and shown no leniency!"

In an attempt to assuage Michinaga's agitation, a lady-in-waiting to the empress dowager approached him and relayed her mistress' comment: "What your lordship says is true, of course, but inasmuch as the empress is also at the Nijō mansion, please do not take too heavy-handed a measure."

The sound of wailing from the former regent's household was loud enough to be heard beyond the middle gates. It was noised about among those in the house that, things being as they were, a departure that evening would be utterly unreasonable. More than anything, for Korechika the empress' presence was a great source of security. Several times Takaie took Korechika's hand, saying, "It will be just as difficult to part no matter how long we wait. Come on, let's show some resolution and leave." Each time, however, their mother would join Korechika's hand firmly with the empress' and, in a state of agitation that belied her usual clearheaded wit, would wail, "No! As long as the empress is here, what can they do to the palace minister? If Korechika were no longer here, I myself would die!" The empress herself had begun to realize that because of her "big sisterly" love for the emperor, hope for the advancement of her family had been dashed, and that power had passed into the hands of another. She could not therefore in good conscience bring herself to urge Korechika on his way to his place of exile, but just gave herself over to tears with the others.

Takaie said to her, "Why should you grieve at this late hour? A year ago I predicted that such a day would come. Now that I think about it, I was just like the tiger moth that flies into the flame, hastening its own demise. It has been the same for you, brother, so don't carry on with your effeminate weeping and wailing at this late hour, disgracing our father's name!" That night, he loaded his cart and resolutely set out for Izumo.

Those guarding the mansion knew that difficulties would preclude Korechika's leaving before the next morning, and they built great watch fires in front of the garden. As they dozed there that night, an unexpected thing happened.

Daylight came like the tense calm that follows a great earthquake. Early that morning, messengers again came from the palace to press the matter, and some Minamoto warriors from the country stole up to the veranda and peeked inside the bamboo blinds. In a state of agitation, one of them dashed to the superintendent of the imperial police and blurted out, "It looks suspicious. . . . The palace minister. . . I mean, the governor-general . . . is nowhere to be seen inside. You see, we should have loaded him on a cart last night, even if we had to bind him hand and foot. Now what will happen to us when the lord regent hears about this?"

The superintendent was stunned. When he announced that he wished to meet with the governor-general, Norimasa emerged and said, without looking the superintendent in the face, as if with a guilty conscience, "My lord is ill and resting. I beg you wait until this evening." Then he slipped inside, making an escape.

When this was reported to the palace, the emperor was still at his evening quarters. Without a trace of agitation in his voice, Michinaga sternly ordered, "Storm the mansion now, search the rafters and break down the inside walls. If the governor-general is nowhere to be found, the imperial police and the soldiers will be held accountable also."

The superintendent answered respectfully, "I shall see to it that all else is done as you command, but it is difficult for us to act with the empress present. They say that she is with child. His majesty might be displeased by any rash action, so I have tended to be rather indulgent about everything."

With no change in expression Michinaga commanded, "I'll take full responsibility for that, and none of you will be blamed. Make sure that the empress is concealed from sight, and then search the house. Don't hold back."

The night before, Korechika had slipped out to bid farewell at his father's grave in Kohata. He was supposed to have returned by morning, but it took longer than expected, and the sun was already high as he made his way back. Thinking that there was nothing for it but to wait until evening, he hid in the house of a woman with whom he was acquainted. In the meantime, the search of the Nijō mansion was underway. Just as Yukikuni had feared, country soldiers went charging up the steps alongside the imperial police, showing no reservation as they cleared the bamboo blinds and curtains out of their way with their swords and halberds, yelling, "Imperial order! . . . Imperial order!" Soldiers were running about from the entrance to the main building searching for Korechika.

The ladies-in-waiting and girls attending the empress did not ordinarily show their faces to such uncouth soldiers. Fearful and weeping, the women clustered about the empress' curtained dais like flower petals quivering in the wind. At the empress' side was Kureha, whose erect posture bespoke her indomitable nature. She had no use for the argument that "such were the times" and loathed Michinaga's having committed such a barbarism at the empress' residence. Should anyone force his way within the curtains, she was determined to protect her highness and conceal her royal countenance from the eyes of any rustic boors. She hardly blinked as she concentrated on every sign from beyond the curtains: the sound of things being toppled, the coarse voices of the men, the shrieking of the ladies-in-waiting.

In the meantime, the secretary of the imperial police, Yukikuni, had climbed into the rafters of the main hall. He had for the most part concluded that Korechika was not in the residence. Rather than help with the search, he stood near the women surrounding the curtained dais to prevent any soldiers from approaching the empress. Kureha was nowhere to be seen, and Yukikuni concluded she must also be inside the curtains. He marveled at the strange turn of events that had brought a lowly functionary like him into the main building of the former regent's household on the day of its greatest crisis, there to be separated by a mere curtain from his lover, who was with the empress.

The search had utterly ravaged the main building, but it had been in vain; Korechika was nowhere to be found in the house. Norimasa's statement that he was supposed to have gone to visit a grave and that he would certainly return by nightfall was relayed to the palace. Just as the shadows of dusk were rendering indistinct the airy spaces in trees on the islet of the pond and in the garden, a single ox cart with a wicker cover entered quietly through the middle gate, right through the tight security. A minor official of the imperial police, clad in a red robe and with a spear in his hand, ran up to the cart and demanded, "Who goes there?" An uncommonly refined voice answered from within, "I am the governor-general, returning from a visit to a grave. Allow me to enter." The author of *A Tale of Flowering Fortunes* describes as follows the appearance of Korechika alighting from the cart in the covered passage leading to the middle gate:

> He seemed to be only about twenty-two or twenty-three: neat in appearance, slightly plump, well featured, and of a fair complexion—perhaps the very picture of the shining Prince Genji. He was wearing three delicate, light gray robes over an undergarment of the same color, and his overrobe and trousers were

the same. Both his accomplishments and his appearance were said to exceed what is usually found among court nobles. Everyone thought it sad that he remained in the cart instead of riding through the gate, as if he alone were showing deference to the empress. It was reported that the Governor-General had returned from Kohata, and an edict came in response from the Palace saying that, since it was already nightfall, he should be well guarded until the Hour of the Hare [about 6:00 A.M.] the next morning, when he should be sent on his way.

Korechika, who had just returned, was astounded at the violence that had left the main building in shambles. At the same time he sensed how irresistible Michinaga's offensive move was and that it showed not the slightest remission in spite of the fact that the empress was residing there.

Throughout that entire night, Korechika and his family bade affectionate farewells to one another, but just as Takaie had said, even after two days the reluctance to part had not abated. Their mother, Kishi, continued to give herself over to weeping, pressing her face into the empress' and Korechika's hands clutched in front of her.

The imperial police were at an utter loss. After reporting several times to the palace, a command finally came from Michinaga: "I don't care if you have to wrest him from the empress' embrace. If an imperial edict appears to be disregarded, it slights the authority of the emperor."

They realized that further hesitation would jeopardize their own positions. The superintendent of the imperial police was perforce about to take it upon himself when Yukikuni stepped forward and said, "I shall assume the task of separating the palace minister from the empress. Please do not give the assignment to anyone else." The superintendent replied, "Well, then, I shall leave it up to you. Whatever you do, don't be timid and bungle it!"

Later, when reflecting back on all this, Yukikuni could not decide what possessed him at that time to volunteer for such an important mission. Perhaps it was his genuine feeling that it would be a sacrilege to expose Kureha's adored mistress to the gaze of another uncouth man.

Yukikuni first approached Norimasa and explained that it would be disadvantageous to the empress as well if they delayed any longer, but the old man apparently had heard such persuasion too often. It was as if his mind had shriveled, no longer capable of prudent judgment.

Yukikuni realized that he could not delay any longer and, pushing his way through the dappled disarray of the robes of wailing ladies-in-waiting, approached the curtain and announced in a loud voice: "Secretary of Imperial Police Tachibana no Yukikuni has come for his lordship the governor-general." There was no response from within; the sound of Kishi's sobbing could be plainly heard. Yukikuni waited for a while, but since there was no answer, he added, "With all due respect, your lordship, this is an imperial edict." As he spoke, he lifted one of the curtains. He could see the black hair of the mother, prostrate with grief, pressed down upon Korechika's and the empress' clasped hands. At the same time he was dazed by a subtle fragrance that came wafting out.

Directly before him, a woman was looking at him quietly, with a steady gaze. He ought to have understood that it was the empress, but he was so overwhelmed by the radiant beauty of that face that for a moment he felt both the dread and the ecstasy of a criminal placed before a bodhisattva. "Please, let go of his hand, I beg of you." Yukikuni's youthful face flushed as if pierced by a strong light. He enunciated his words in a dream-like stupor and, taking Korechika by the hand, tried to make him stand. Kishi, clinging to Korechika's waist, rose totteringly with the two men, and then stroked Korechika's trousers with both hands as if she were blind.

The empress made no attempt to conceal her tearless face with a fan, as noblewomen were wont to do at such times. She remained sitting and did not release Korechika's hand even after he had stood up, and was pulled into a kneeling position. Like a moonflower rising from the thinly layered, light red undergarments surrounded by a deep purple outer robe, her lustrous white face was slightly raised to look up at her brother. It was for but a moment that Yukikuni saw the empress' face, but he had so lost his composure that, for all he knew, it might have been an eternity. When he finally succeeded in pulling Korechika outside the curtains, he felt as if he were in a waking dream. He could still feel pressed into his palm the cool and uncrushable petal-like softness of the empress' hand, from which he had wrested Korechika's. At the same time, he could also see the pink, fleshy face of a woman, her eyes firmly set and fairly bursting with anger, standing and spreading her sleeve to cover the empress. When he realized that it was Kureha, the woman pledged to be his mate for life, he felt drained of power, as if he were sliding into the very depths of hell.

Although Kureha had been at the empress' side constantly up to that time, she was worried about the pallid color of her highness' face and had slipped outside the curtains briefly to prepare a medicinal broth. Upon returning, she was surprised beyond measure to find her lover, Yukikuni, attempting to free Korechika's hand from the empress' grasp by prying it loose from her fingers. Instinctively she went to protect the empress, crying, "How dare you!"

Kishi would not listen to anyone who tried to stop her. Half-crazed, she joined Korechika in a cart, wailing plaintively, "I'll go with him . . . at least as far as Yamazaki. . . ." They were unable to force the empress' mother from the cart and decided to send her back somehow or other after they were beyond the capital. Under the imposing guard of the imperial police, the party escorting Korechika to his place of exile left through the middle gate and headed toward Yamazaki.

The empress stood in the ravaged side room, watching transfixed as Korechika's cart drove off. At length she returned to the curtained dais in the main building. She had Kureha fetch a pair of scissors and tried to cut her body-length, glossy black hair. "Your Highness, you must not be so rash! Think of the prince you are carrying. . . ." Her nurses, Jijū and Chūshō, clung to her arms, and Kureha likewise made a determined effort to stop her, but the empress' resolve was firm. After cutting off more than a foot of hair, she bunched it together and said tersely, "Take this to the palace, and have Ukon no Naishi present it to his majesty."

After receiving the lock of hair that night, the emperor's grief was such that he clutched the liquid-cool, heavy tress to his breast and wept until daybreak. All the next day, he refused to go to the throne.

Neither did the emperor wish to see the empress dowager or Michinaga. When he thought of the cruel blow dealt to the empress and to her father's household by an imperial order that did not in the least represent his wishes, his nights became sleepless.

Seeing how profoundly shaken the emperor was by the empress' remonstrance, even Michinaga was sorry that his medicine had been too effective, and he changed Korechika's and Takaie's places of exile from Tsukushi [Kyushu] and Izumo to the nearby provinces of Harima and Tajima. After remaining by Korechika's side for half of the journey, Kishi finally gave up and returned to the capital, but upon seeing that the empress' locks were shortened, she again collapsed in tears.

In contrast to the rundown appearance of the now masterless Nijō residence, where the empress had quietly secluded herself, the daily stream of carts through the gate of Michinaga's Tsuchimikado Palace seemed endless, and the sycophantic voices of his visitors floated on the air like the twittering of a flock of birds.

Toward the end of the fifth month, when people of the capital were beginning to forget the uproar, Kureha finally took a day's leave from the empress' court and went to Yukikuni's house.

Yukikuni's house was in the middle of a block not far from the office of the imperial police.

Although Kureha had informed Yukikuni ahead of time that she would stop by on her way back from visiting a temple, when she was shown inside a servant boy said, "My lord is now at the riding grounds breaking horses. Please wait for a while." Yukikuni's parents had died two or three years earlier in a smallpox epidemic. His mother was the daughter of an assistant commander in the provincial government of Owari, and the entire inheritance from her family had been left to him. For a young, single military officer, he was therefore rather well off, and had a house full of servants.

In the guest room, built to imitate the palace style of architecture, along with a sword there was on display a large overrobe of yellow-green figured cloth, apparently from Michinaga as a reward for his recent meritorious services in seeing Korechika off to exile. Looking at it, Kureha was gripped by an unpleasant premonition as she recalled the day when Yukikuni entered the curtained dais in the Nijō mansion, but she dismissed those feelings and looked out into the rear courtyard from interstices in the lattice on the north side.

An entire large, vacant lot there had been turned into a riding ground, with cherry trees and maples planted in every corner. Yukikuni, the sleeves of his hunting robe gathered up, was riding an overly spirited sorrel. He drew in the reins of the unruly steed as it was about to rear, and went racing about the grounds as he broke the animal. A burly young man—one of the horsekeepers—ran behind in the dust, now falling back when it seemed he was about to be kicked by the restive horse, now running closer again. The usual gentleness had disappeared from the face of Yukikuni, who was ably riding the raging horse; his perspiring face had reddened from his forehead to his firmly set cheeks. Kureha's heart unexpectedly raced as she looked at the gallant manliness of her lover. For some time she continued to lean against the lattice, watching the mounted figure of Yukikuni as he rode away and then back again. Perhaps because he was concentrating so intently on drilling the horse, however, he never once looked in her direction.

When Kureha returned to her seat after a half hour or so had passed, the long twilight hours of summer were already about to turn into night. Yukikuni, who had washed himself at the bathhouse and changed clothes, entered, the color of polishing powder still on his cheeks.

"I'm sorry I kept you waiting. . . . I've been breaking that restive horse for the lord regent." As he apologized, he sat close to Kureha and asked, "Aren't you hungry? You're on your way back, aren't you, from a pilgrimage to Iwashimizu?" Instead of being so solicitous, Kureha wished he would embrace her roughly and run his fingers through her hair. Since she could not make any such request, she decided to dine with him, and mentioned some sweetfish she had had delivered to the kitchen. "Sweetfish? Thanks, that's quite a treat. I'll have them cooked right away, and then let's eat."

Both of them were somehow too embarrassed to talk about their unexpected meeting during the great arrest a month earlier.

With the sweetfish as a side dish, Kureha offered milky white saké to Yukikuni. After two or three cups he finally asked, "How has the empress been since then? I have been worried that all the uproar might have been bad for her in her condition. I hear that she cut her hair...."

"That's right. She took up the scissors herself. But actually, she only cut a bit off the end, so you wouldn't know just to look at her. But I hear that his majesty really took it to heart when he saw what she had done, and that the places of exile for the palace minister and the middle counselor were changed because of that...."

"That's probably true. Knowing the lord regent, he probably intended to have all supporting male relatives out of the way before the empress gives birth to a prince. Ordinarily, he seems to be a broad-minded sort of person who isn't fussy about particulars, but once he makes up his mind to do something, he doesn't deviate from that. The truth is, the only one the lord regent fears right now is the empress. There's no telling what kinds of terrible things might be in store for her highness, and the danger is greater than just false mediums. You, too, must be careful."

Kureha nodded in wholehearted agreement as she listened to Yukikuni's kind advice. Then she said almost boastfully, "You saw the empress too, then, didn't you? Wouldn't you agree that she is a peerless beauty?"

At that, Yukikuni's face flushed around his eyes as he stammered an answer. "There was a lot of glare, and I don't really remember her face. The only thing that remains in my mind is your angry face. . . ."

Kureha returned to the Nijō mansion that night. Although Yukikuni had seemed so robust and fearless as he trained the horse on the grounds, when the two of them met alone, he seemed fatigued and physically unresponsive. They did not share their usual rapture, and Kureha felt that something was lacking. In the cart on the way back to Nijō, she muttered to herself, "I wonder if there's something wrong with him physically. Tonight he didn't say a word about our wedding day, even though he always makes a point of talking about it. . . ."

On the eighth day of the sixth month, a fire broke out in the west wing of the Nijō mansion where the empress was staying. The great mansion that former Regent Michitaka had maintained with such refined taste was reduced to ashes in one night during the absence of its masters, Korechika and Takaie.

It was in the middle of summer, when there was no need to keep fires for warmth. It was said that it was probably due to the inattentiveness of a low-ranking servant, that a lamplight was placed too close to a paper screen or something. But it was also furtively whispered about that someone had complied with Michinaga's wishes that—should an opportunity present itself —the empress' life be taken, and had intentionally set the fire knowing where her chamber was. Such rumors were passed about from the palace all the way down to the market place.

When Michinaga received the news, he went to the imperial palace for an audience with his majesty in spite of the late hour. The regent himself seemed relieved to report, "Fortunately, the empress was safely removed to the mansion of Takashina no Akinobu." Actually, even during the worst of the conflagration Michinaga had been worried and inquired several times about the safety of the empress, but those who were disposed to think the worst of him rumored that his only concern was whether or not his plan had succeeded.

The flames had spread rapidly. By the time Kureha became aware of them, an infernal blaze like a red lotus blossom was creeping closer to the curtained dais where the empress was sleeping.

The sound of wood splitting, the screams of people running about in confusion, the crash of things falling over . . . all were accompanied by a life-and-death urgency not felt in the previous disturbance at the mansion. A suffocating smoke and the odor of burning enveloped the main building. The ladies-in-waiting quite forgot themselves as they scrambled to find an escape. Nurse Chūshō and Kureha put a thin silk cloth over the empress' hair, and, standing on either side of her, each took a hand and tried to escape along the veranda toward the east wing. Suddenly, a suspicious-looking smoke began to billow up from beneath the floor, blocking their way. "Oh, it has spread to here!" cried the confused nurse, and she came to a standstill. Then, as if disgorged from the dense, billowing smoke, a dark, masked figure suddenly approached, wrested the empress' hand from Chūshō's grasp, and stood in front of them, blocking the way out, seemingly to force the half-conscious empress to return to the inferno. Kureha screamed frantically, "What are you doing? This is the empress! This is an outrage. . . . Don't you see there's nothing back there but flames?" She tried to free the empress' hand from the man she believed to be an ally; however, not only did his vise-like grip not yield, but without saying a word he pushed Kureha away, hitting her head hard against one of the outside pillars.

Her voice choked with smoke, Kureha cried out, "The empress . . . somebody . . . save the empress!" In her half-dazed mind, she thought it strange that none of the many ladies-in-waiting and attendants who ought to have been at her highness' side were around. When she again grasped the pillar and lifted her reeling head, she could see another dark figure wordlessly approach the previous giant of a man and, effortlessly freeing the empress' outer robe from his grasp, carry her at his side as if receiving a fancy package.

The big man silently fell down onto the floorboards before the approaching flames, seemingly struck down by the latter dark figure who, coughing in the smoke, carried the empress with utmost care and approached the balustrade where Kureha was. "That was close. . . ." muttered the man. When Kureha could finally see his face, she let out a startled cry: "Yukikuni!"

Kureha's voice had become hoarse from the smoke, but she crawled up to Yukikuni and clung to his feet. However, he seemed not to recognize her then. Brutally kicking away her hands, he went to the balustrade and shouted, "Secretary of the Imperial Police Yukikuni has rescued the empress. There's no time to lose. Someone down there make ready to receive her."

He shouted this announcement two or three times, and faces filled with awe and excitement gathered beneath the balustrade. The superintendent of the imperial police, who had just arrived, yelled back, "You've done well, Yukikuni. Get her highness inside these curtains before the roof caves in!" Yukikuni gently set the empress, her eyes closed like a Buddhist image, down in a five-colored, figured cloth spread out by five or six minor attendants.

"Do you have hold of her?"

"I have her."

"You jump down, too, and be quick! The eaves are about to come down!"

"All right." Before he could say more, Yukikuni jumped from the balustrade. At that moment he thought he heard a woman's voice behind him calling, "Yukikuni!" He realized it was Kureha and recalled with uncanny vividness that it was her small but strong hands that had gripped his feet only a few moments before. Kureha had been left behind in the blaze! As soon as he realized that, he tried to go again toward the stairs. "Yukikuni, are you mad? The whole wing is on fire!" Almost simultaneously with the superintendent's frantic shout, there was a terrific rumble and the crash of a falling beam, and Yukikuni had to dodge a lightning-like pillar of flame that fell right in front of him.

"Kureha is dead. . . . She's in the middle of those flames." The thoughts screamed in his mind as he stared vacantly up at the main building of the Nijō mansion, now burning furiously and scorching the summer night sky like a colossal beacon fire. He had acted to the full extent of his powers to protect the life of the empress. He had not been party to any specific information but sensed intuitively that the defenseless empress, together with the child she was carrying, would doubtless be subjected to Michinaga's plots to eliminate them. Perhaps it had been the instinctive sensibilities of one in love. To Yukikuni's mind, such a beautiful person, left alone and without support, must not have to endure further unhappiness, much less be killed. To prevent such an outcome he would willingly risk his life. He realized only too well that his love must ever remain unrequited, and yet in the resplendent beauty of the empress, who had looked at him with such dignity on the day he entered the dais to arrest Korechika, Yukikuni sensed the summation of all feminine virtues, a fountain of allure one glimpse of which would captivate any man's soul. After sleeping with Kureha on the evening not long before when she had called on him, an emptiness remained in his heart as if he had been embracing an earthenware doll. On the day of the arrest he had taken home with him a silver comb with several silk-like strands of glossy black hair wrapped around it that had been caught in the cord of his robe. He kept them next to his bosom as a priceless treasure, taking them out time and time again to stare at them wistfully.

What a stroke of good fortune that he had been able to hold the empress in his arms and walk through the flames, thereby thwarting the plans of a villain who had very nearly succeeded in robbing her of her life. Her lissome form was visible beneath layered robes so heavily scented as to make one swoon; she was breathing deeply, and the sensation of her robust, pulsating life almost made Yukikuni forget his own fear of death. Even if he had fallen into the flames as he carried the empress, his dying thoughts would have been ones of ecstasy, like the bliss of being greeted into paradise by a bodhisattva.

It was only after Yukikuni had accompanied the empress' cart to the mansion of her maternal uncle, Takashina no Akinobu, and returned later in the evening that he learned Kureha was alive and safe. As soon as he finally had time to breathe, remorse for having abandoned Kureha began to weigh on him heavily. He stood at the bottom of the stairs to the main building, eyes bloodshot from soot, staring reproachfully at the first rays of the early morning sky.

The ladies-in-waiting were being sent off in carts one after another. They were disheveled, their hair pulled back behind their ears, and they were walking with the hems of their divided skirts pulled up. Yukikuni lacked the courage to look for Kureha among the sooty, unrecognizable figures descending the stairs.

"Yukikuni!" At that voice, he turned his vacant stare to the top of the stairs. There stood Kureha, the left shoulder of her robe singed to a yellowish brown, her hair in specter-like disarray, looking down on him as silently as a spider.

"Oh, Kureha! Thank goodness you're alive!" Yukikuni shouted out, and was about to ascend the stairs, but he was repelled by her stillness and the forbidding look in her eyes. "Yukikuni, I know very well what your feelings are. Please consider our relationship ended as of this moment." So saying, she turned her back and disappeared quietly within the bamboo blinds. Never had the view of Kureha with her back turned to him projected such a majestic air. With one foot on the stairs, as if pinned in place, Yukikuni looked at her retreating figure, which was brimming with a steady anger.

That day, Yukikuni was summoned to Michinaga's mansion, where he was praised highly for taking expedient measures to save the empress. "If anything had happened to the empress, especially following Korechika's and Takaie's exile, I wouldn't have been able to face his majesty." Michinaga ordered Yukikuni thereafter to continue maintaining a keen watch over the safety and welfare of the empress.

Kureha continued to serve at the empress' side as before. In spite of Yukikuni's having saved the empress at the moment when life and death hung in the balance, the sorrow and bitterness of his having paid no heed to her own desperate screams hardened into something that lay coiled in her heart like a black serpent.

Yukikuni himself was deeply ashamed of his callous behavior toward Kureha and made no attempt to approach her again. Since the day he had set eyes on the empress, Kureha seemed like a faint star next to the moon, and as long as she was safe and sound, he did not experience such unbearable grief at breaking relations with her. For Kureha, however, Yukikuni was the first man with whom she had been intimate, and she had believed unquestioningly in his devotion. The shock that night was thus all the more cruel. She tried to reconsider, thinking that she ought actually to be able to feel a selfless joy in the fact that her lover risked his life to save her beloved mistress. And yet her bitterness toward Yukikuni only deepened. A side effect of those feelings was an occasional irrational envy toward the empress whom she had attended with such care. It was the envy toward a woman who had stolen her man's heart.

The empress was not in the least aware of the fierce flame of malice that was growing daily within Kureha and continued to lavish affection on her and to trust her implicitly.

Even the adversity of having been forcibly separated from her blood relations, of her house burning down, and of losing her mother to illness in the tenth month of that year did not in the least diminish the empress' grace and refinement. On the sixteenth day of the twelfth month of that year, Princess Shūshi was safely brought into the world.

The one most disappointed that the child was not a prince was the empress' grandfather, Naritada, but there is no doubt that the one most relieved was Michinaga. He had been fervently praying that Empress Teishi would not give birth to a son before his own eldest daughter, Shōshi, could be presented at court as a lady-in-waiting.

A Tale of Flowering Fortunes gives the following description:

> She gave birth to a Princess. At first she thought that, had the choice been hers, it would have been so promising and joyous to have borne a son, yet when she reflected further on the unpleasant situation at court, she realized how pleased she was. At the orders of His Majesty, Ukon no Naishi went to assist in the bathing ceremonies. The situation being what it was, she was nervous and apprehensive, but she honored the imperial command and went.

From the description of the dread of Ukon no Naishi, lady-in-waiting in attendance to the emperor himself, to go to the empress and assist in the bathing ceremonies of the new princess because "the situation being what it was, she was nervous and apprehensive," one can see how the influence of Regent Michinaga extended even to those close to his majesty. This passage betrays the real intentions of its author to try to present the household of the Buddha-Hall lord (Michinaga) as the epitome of all virtues. From the fact that even a description written by an insider loyal to Michinaga did not gloss over the matter, it would appear that the court did not bother itself much with expenses related to the birth of the first princess.

Nevertheless, with the birth of the princess, the emperor's feelings of love for the empress grew even stronger. In spite of her having cut her hair as a gesture of renouncing the world, in the sixth month of the following year she returned to court with the princess and renewed her intimacy with the emperor.

Chapter Five ～

The description in *A Tale of Flowering Fortunes* implies that it was at the urging of her grandfather, Takashina no Naritada, that Empress Teishi resolved to take the little princess and return to the imperial palace.

Naritada mourned the loss of his daughter, Kishi, and the grandsons on whom he had so counted, Korechika and Takaie, were in exile. Though he was experiencing disappointment as only an old man can, he nevertheless remained resolute in his prayers for the revival of his family's fortunes. He was disappointed that Empress Teishi's first child was a princess, but took comfort in the fact that no other child had been born to the emperor by any of his ladies-in-waiting and that, as long as the emperor and empress had an intimate relationship, a prince was certain to be born eventually. He spurred on the reluctant empress, insisting that the incantations and prayers he had been offering were already showing signs of efficacy. Of course, Naritada's urging did not seem entirely unreasonable, but the empress' decision to return to the palace and present herself to the emperor after more than a year's absence—and in spite of having renounced the world by cutting her hair—was not solely the result of her grandfather's advice; the account in *A Tale of False Fortunes* suggests that her love for the emperor helped her to bury her shame. There it is recorded:

> *His Majesty was extremely vexed that the Empress showed no interest in returning to court. He no longer had the ladies then serving in the Shōkōden and Kokiden Palaces attend him in the evenings, nor did he join them in any of their splendid diversions. When it grew dark, he would quickly retreat to his evening quarters, where he would spend the night writing letters to the Empress and pining*

for her. When the Lord Regent saw this, he found it disturbing and reported it to the Empress Dowager.

Michinaga's real intention was to use the empress' renunciation of the world as an excellent opportunity to prevent the revival of her intimacy with the emperor. No matter how much the emperor yearned for his consort and recommended that she return to court, Michinaga erected a barrier, insisting that it would be an affront to the gods and the buddhas for anyone who had once become a nun to resume her former status as empress. There was no one at court who would venture to carry out the emperor's wishes in the face of Michinaga's then solid authority.

> *Even compared with other emperors, he was not at all lacking. Beginning with his features and his disposition, he was in all things felicitously endowed, and therefore people served him with devotion, saying that a degenerate age did not deserve to have such a ruler.*

As this description in *A Tale of False Fortunes* indicates, Emperor Ichijō was second only to Emperor Murakami as a young aristocrat of upright character. Moreover, since he was the favorite son of the Higashisanjō empress dowager, Michinaga's benefactress, even the regent was unable to manipulate the position of the throne. What Michinaga desired was that Empress Teishi not give birth to a male heir before his eldest daughter reached the appropriate age to be introduced at court as an imperial consort and bear the emperor's son.

The empress dowager also sensed what Michinaga's intentions were, and for a time likewise recommended that Empress Teishi not return to court with the new princess. One day, however, she was surprised to see how emaciated the emperor looked.

After the emperor's briefing on affairs of state, the empress dowager met with him in the upper quarters of the Kokiden Palace. She looked with pity on his face, on his downcast eyes set above wan, gaunt cheeks. "I have been relieved to hear that you were not ill, but you do not seem to be in good spirits. What is wrong? It saddens me to see you like this; I have no one to rely on but your majesty."

Upon hearing this, the emperor cast his eyes down even further, then raised them brimming with tears. "Mother, I did not want to say this as long as you are alive, but . . . somehow I feel depressed, and I can't be certain that I won't precede you in death. . . . I'm thinking that perhaps the time has come that I should abdicate the throne to my cousin, the crown prince." Even as he was speaking, he wiped with his sleeve the tears that were trickling down his face.

"Well, now, what nonsense you speak! Surely no one will agree to the abdication of someone in the prime of his life, like you. But, if something is not to your liking, why hesitate to confide in your mother? If you just talk about it, I shall see to it that your mind is put at ease. . . ." As the empress dowager spoke, she became aware that something pensive and listless at the depths of the emperor's heart was projecting itself onto her. "What you really wish to talk about is the empress, isn't it? I shall see to it that the empress is reinstated at court, along with the little princess, so you mustn't speak of such things as abdication."

Having thus remonstrated with the emperor, the empress dowager summoned Michinaga and explained that if they did not now install the empress at court the emperor might decide to abdicate, and that even if he did not go that far, it would be a matter of grave concern if he should ruin his health. She urged him therefore to reinstate the empress at court.

Michinaga began to take positive steps to reinstate the empress, though he was secretly reluctant to do so. At the urging both of the empress dowager and Michinaga—and particularly moved by a letter from the emperor declaring his love for her—the empress finally resolved to return.

The empress had been absent from court for rather a long time, and she had to arrange for things in a manner that would not invite derision: suitable apparel for her ladies-in-waiting, and the rites for the new princess' presentation. The empress had lost any influential backing; there was, in fact, no one to collect for her the income that ought to be due an imperial consort—income that would enable her to provide such necessities. Things did not proceed to her satisfaction. She had silk and figured cloth brought in from the manors and tried to make do with it.

When the day arrived, Michinaga summoned all of the court officials and ordered them to arrange themselves in a procession suitable to receive the empress. A person close to the regent remarked, "It is unbecoming for one who has renounced the world to be reinstated at court. Certainly there is no need for you to show such solicitousness in these matters. . . ." But Michinaga replied, "No, we mustn't try his majesty's feelings further." He received Teishi with all the solemnity he had formerly shown her. People praised his handling of things, saying, "What a broad-minded, generous man he is!" It was only Imperial Police Yukikuni, following the procession as the one chosen to guard the empress, who saw through to Michinaga's inward displeasure and sensed the danger that lay ahead for her highness.

The evening of the empress' return to court are described in *A Tale of False Fortunes* in roughly the following manner.

Upon their arrival at court, it was the empress dowager who came to meet them first of all. "At last, we are able to meet," she said as she took the little princess into her arms. She saw how very charming and chubby the little child was and smiled with pity, thinking, "If only the times were better." The little princess was not at all shy of the unfamiliar woman, and babbled endearingly. The empress dowager was convinced that even this infant recognized blood relationship.

In view of all that had happened since the previous year, the empress maintained a certain reserve. As the empress dowager addressed her and looked on her countenance for the first time in a long time, she did not wonder that his majesty should consider her quite without equal.

At length the emperor arrived. His handsome face was radiant with a smile as he looked at the little princess in the nurse's arms. He sighed in spite of himself, "Ah, to think that half a year has passed without my seeing this darling child." He felt sorry that the child was not a boy, for then he could have treated the empress with greater dignity.

The empress dowager took the little princess and returned to her quarters. After that the emperor met with the empress, whom he had not seen in nearly a year and a half. At first he feigned an air of reservation, seemingly somewhat embarrassed that the passionate tone of his daily letters and poems to her had reached the point of distraction. The empress' hair was even longer and more luxuriant than before. Although there was nothing about her to suggest she had become a nun, at first she maintained decorum and placed a screen between them.

Before she knew it, the emperor had removed the screen. As he looked at her face illuminated by a lamp, fond memories at once welled up in his heart, and his discretion melted away like light snow. He pulled her close to his side as if to wrap himself in her smooth skin, which was like glossy white silk draped over her frame. Restraining tears, he spent an entire night in an agitated state of mind.

The empress herself was helpless against a powerful resurgence of feelings for the emperor, who during their long separation had become quite an adult, his voice and frame manly. On the pretext of wanting to have the little princess at his side where he could watch her (though in reality he wished only to be with the empress), he decided that mother and daughter should stay in the apartments of the empress' household. He himself went there every morning and had their meals brought to them there.

Though he realized that the regent and all of the related nobles in the Shōkōden and Kokiden Palaces would not be pleased, the emperor did not demur at such considerations and continued to go to the empress.

It was whispered about disparagingly among men and women at the palace that it was unbecoming to treat a nun with such pomp and splendor, but Michinaga dismissed such complaints nonchalantly. "When a man becomes infatuated with a woman, he will always go through a phase of caring nothing about honor or about the opinion of society. Until now, his majesty was a mere boy. This passion that we see in him now is just an indication that he has reached full manhood. If he didn't have at least that much spirit about him, how could he be called the lord of all under heaven? I myself am rather pleased to see it."

Michinaga clearly perceived a certain defiance toward himself in the emperor's unreserved affection for the empress.

The emperor seemed prepared to defend his consort from all criticism. He felt apprehensive about having her remain in the apartments of the empress' household and before long moved her to a building directly connected to the Seiryōden Palace, where he could visit her even during the day between affairs of state, and where he could go on his own at night and return at daybreak.

He no longer frequented the Kokiden and Shōkōden Palaces and did not even send letters.

For nearly a year thereafter, he never failed to go to the empress at night. Soon she was once again with child.

She had suffered from morning sickness during her previous pregnancy, but this time her condition was much worse. She was barely able to eat at all and ended up returning to her parental home, much to the disappointment of the emperor. If possible, he would have liked for her to give birth to a prince at the palace, but even he was not permitted to break precedent to such a degree.

Within the bedchamber on the evening before she was to return to her parents' home, the empress looked steadfastly at the emperor and said, gently stroking his slightly disheveled sidelocks as a mother or elder sister might do, "If I have a prince, I'll return as soon as possible. In the meantime please try to get along with your mother and with the regent." The empress was ashamed that, in spite of having become a nun, she had continued in conjugal relations and had even become pregnant. And yet her affection for the emperor exceeded her shame, and she found it difficult to part. When she had first come to the palace he was still just a boy playing with tops, but now he had become quite a man, able resolutely to keep both anger and patience within himself, and had become a worthy object of her love.

"No matter what anyone says, you must not believe it unless it comes directly from my own mouth. Even my mother cannot correctly relay what I feel for you. . . ." With that, the emperor embraced her so tightly that she could hardly breathe. His arms were full of the power of newly attained manhood.

Next to the curtained dais, like a coiled white serpent, Kureha was intently listening to the pledges between the emperor and empress, who were like lovers in hiding from the world.

The author of *A Tale of False Fortunes* implies that the outcome would have been much better had the unhappy parting of Kureha and Yukikuni at the time of the fire really been the end of their relationship:

In the spring, Kureha went to the country. Upon visiting the cottage of the nun under whose charge she had been placed, she found that she had come at a good time: the old woman was preparing to leave on a pilgrimage to Hase. She said that the peonies were in full bloom along the roofed steps leading to the Temple and asked Kureha if she would not accompany her. Kureha was delighted and readily consented. They arrived at a place called Tsubaichi, where they spent the night in a suitable lodge, and climbed the stairs to the temple on the next day.

The spring day was resplendent. Though it was an arduous climb up the long, roofed stairway, the sight of peonies in full bloom on both sides was indescribable: red, white, and pink—the very essence of the season. Kureha began to feel somewhat refreshed in spirit, as if she were strolling through Buddha's paradise. The nun said that it was through the providence of Lord Buddha that they were even able to behold such a sight; continuing up the steep steps, she repeated mantras until she was out of breath. As the daughter of a Shinto shamaness, Kureha was unaccustomed to invoking Buddha's mercy, but to her dispirited heart, still bitter from her parting with Yukikuni, the unusual sight of the peonies in full bloom seemed glorious and was a comfort to her.

Toward evening they went up into the temple. The

lamps were lit, and they listened to the priest chant sutras.
The nun's quarters were immediately to the right of the
image of Buddha, owing perhaps to the Regent's influence
having become so pervasive. Having finished her evening
recitation of the sutras, the old woman was fatigued and
dozed off sitting up. Unable to sleep, Kureha went out to
the passageway. A misty moon was high in the sky and the
air was thick with the fragrance of flowers. The charming
scene, veiled in spring mists, did not seem at all like that
of a mountain temple, and it was utterly captivating.

Kureha was surprised when someone came up from
behind and gently embraced her shoulders. It was Yuki-
kuni. Although both a sadness and an unforgettable bit-
terness immediately filled her heart as his shadowed face
abruptly drew close to hers, it was nevertheless difficult
for her to move from the spot. She thought she might be
dreaming and said, flustered, "What are you doing here?"
She tried to shake her shoulder free, but Yukikuni did not
yield and took her in his embrace.

"I said nothing at the time when you denounced me,
but my heart has grown heavier since then. When I heard
that you had gone with the nun on a pilgrimage to Hase,
I decided to throw myself at Kannon's mercy. I set aside
the duties of office and followed you here." It was not
that her contempt and bitterness were alleviated at hear-
ing these words; it was rather as if a heretofore unknown
physical impulse took over. She yielded to Yukikuni's entic-
ing and slept with him in a room far removed from the
image of Buddha.

What were Yukikuni's intentions in reviving his intimacy
with Kureha? Was it that his conscience required him to make
amends for having wronged her at the time of the fire at the
Nijō mansion? More likely, it was because of the peculiar sen-
sitivity of one in love: he must have felt apprehensive that some
evil might befall the empress if dark resentments continued to
fester in Kureha's tenacious heart, through which coursed the
blood of a medium.

It was through her pledge to Yukikuni, the first man she had loved, that Kureha had come to know physical intimacy, and for that reason he had an absolute power over her. Though she stubbornly refused to forgive him completely, she was unable to reject his advances.

Thus, beginning with the pilgrimage to Hase, the amorous relationship between Yukikuni and Kureha was rekindled.

Nowhere does *A Tale of False Fortunes* reveal whether this revival of the love affair resulted from the natural passions in Yukikuni's heart, or whether the old nun—at Michinaga's command, to satisfy some end—had contrived to bring the two young people together. Since it was Michinaga who had worked behind the scenes to bring Yukikuni and Kureha together initially, I think it would be natural for this story if the regent worked secretly to bring about this reunion at Hase as well. That such gaps occur here and there is one obvious flaw in the writing.

An Edo-period author writing in a pseudoclassical style would not be likely to create such inconsistencies, and in that light it is quite conceivable that *A Tale of False Fortunes* is the rather inept scribblings of a woman who lived toward the end of the Monarchical Age or the beginning of the Kamakura period.

Korechika and Takaie were pardoned from their exiles and returned to the capital. Though they remained distanced from the seats of power, they nevertheless were given offices worthy of their lineage. This probably occurred less than a year after Empress Teishi gave birth to Princess Shūshi. There are discrepancies in the various records concerning the timing of their return, but it is reasonable to assume that the empress' having borne the first imperial child, though a princess, was only the ostensible reason for the pardon; in reality it could only have occurred after Michinaga felt assured that political power was securely in his own grasp and that he would not have to yield one inch.

For one thing, Michinaga's suppression of Korechika and Takaie had been too harsh. Perhaps feeling cautioned lest public sympathies tilt toward the two brothers, the regent even gave Korechika a position corresponding in status to minister.

Nevertheless, that they formerly belonged to the opposition—combined with the fact that their sister was the mother of the first imperial daughter—worked against them. And it was not only for Korechika and Takaie that things were difficult; there were local officials and nobles who, out of diffidence toward Michinaga, intentionally neglected to supply the provisions to which the empress was entitled for her maintenance when, for example, she returned to her parental home.

As mentioned previously, the account in *A Tale of Flowering Fortunes* was written as a sort of panegyric to the household of Michinaga. There he is portrayed as not bearing the slightest grudge toward the empress' brothers for their past antagonism. According to that account, the regent personally furnished carts and arranged for a cortege for the empress' comings and goings, and Korechika felt obliged and embarrassed at Michinaga's thoughtful attentiveness to such details. However, it is apparent from other sections that such things were only superficial kindnesses. It is recorded, for example, that the emperor himself hesitated, because of Michinaga, to send messengers to the empress. The author of *A Tale of Flowering Fortunes* writes as though everyone were deferential toward Michinaga because he was a magnanimous and broad-minded man of wealth and influence. But nobles were keenly perceptive of the will of an absolute ruler and would not do anything to provoke his displeasure.

Beginning with Korechika's return to the capital, the author of *A Tale of False Fortunes*—who had up to that point followed many of the accounts in the other work—clearly began to take a very different course.

This change is noticeable after the decline of the former regent's household, in the section in the earlier work known as "Radiant Fujitsubo," which describes the installment at court of Michinaga's eldest daughter, Shōshi, later known as Jōtōmon'in. *A Tale of Flowering Fortunes* describes the beautiful appearance of the young lady, who was twelve years old at the time. It praises her clever personality and portrays as perfectly natural that the emperor's special affection should be focused on the new lady in her dazzling robes and appurtenances. Actually, Michinaga probably had more refined tastes than any previous head of the Fujiwara clan, and one can easily imagine the sumptuous results of his efforts to adorn Shōshi's surroundings to charm the heart of the emperor. From its earliest sections, *A Tale of False Fortunes* records Michinaga's diligence in collecting information about those aspects of the empress' personality that so captivated the emperor. The regent certainly did not neglect the most meticulous preparations in this first step toward the realization of a long-cherished wish.

From the time His Majesty crossed the bridge to the Fujitsubo Pavilion, the building was filled with the fragrance of an unusual sort of incense. It was impossible to identify it, but somehow it permeated him and was quite unlike fragrances anywhere else. Even such things as boxes of combs and inkstone cases left casually lying about . . . not one was of the ordinary sort, and His Majesty looked carefully at each of them. He had come to visit Shōshi early in the morning, and he was delighted by everything in her quarters. Though tender in age, the ladies-in-waiting were also beautiful in appearance and trim in deportment, and he thought he would like to raise the little princess (Princess Shūshi) in such a manner. All the ladies who had been with him until then were now grown up, but these were still very young. He lavished attention on them with the familiarity one would show a beloved younger sister.

It does not explicitly say so in this description from *A Tale of Flowering Fortunes,* but the implication is that Teishi was no match for the charms of Shōshi, who attracted the emperor like the freshness of spring's first blossoms.

On the surface, at least, this was no doubt the atmosphere that prevailed in the imperial women's quarters. The emperor could not afford to make an enemy of Michinaga, and it is hardly likely he would have shown displeasure with the innocent actress placed in the middle of the sumptuous stage the regent had furnished. When he was in the Fujitsubo Pavilion, the emperor was no doubt obligated to play the role of a male doll worthy of Shōshi.

At about the same time as the new lady's splendid presentation at court, Teishi gave birth to Atsuyasu, the first imperial prince. This occurred after she had taken temporary residence at Imperial Steward Taira no Narimasa's rather shabby mansion, which lacked even the four-pillared roofed gates then standard at houses of the aristocracy. Several years previously the household of the former regent was at the height of its glory, but now the extent of the change defied imagination.

Had his heart been fickle and easily seduced by anything new and showy, the emperor might have switched his affection to Shōshi at first sight and never given further thought to Teishi. And yet, no matter how clever Shōshi might have been at that time, she was a mere girl of twelve years. It is not likely that her body had matured to the point that true conjugal relations would have been safely possible. His affection for Teishi—with whom the now twenty-year-old emperor had been deeply intimate for nearly ten years and who had gently directed him in the manner of an elder sister and raised him to manhood—could not have been so easily moved by the appearance of Shōshi on the scene. Such a scenario was rendered all the less probable by Teishi's being the mother of his children: his darling prince and princess. Even if he was moved to love Shōshi as a pretty little girl, it is unthinkable that his long-standing affection for Teishi faded in the least. The author of *A Tale of False Fortunes* was probably of a mind similar to mine and, though perhaps tending somewhat to exaggeration, wished to portray the emperor's constant and loving attachment to his first empress:

The Emperor felt uneasy when it was determined that the Lady of the Fujitsubo Pavilion be elevated to Empress and that she who had occupied that position be called "Empress Consort." It was unprecedented in any previous reign for there to be two empresses at the same time. The First Prince (Prince Atsuyasu) now lacked backing. The Emperor had hoped that the Prince's mother might enjoy a secure position and that the Prince would thereby find great favor with society. But such hopes had been dashed. It occurred to him at times that if this had been during the age of the former Regent, the glory and renown of the

Prince would be praised by every tongue. At such times the Emperor regretted it as an unpardonable sin against his son not to have kept the Lord Governor-General [Korechika] in the regency after the death of Lord Awata [Michikane]. Combined with his tendency to self-censure was his sore longing for Teishi, who was living separately but whose form and features were always before him like an apparition. He even yearned to go wandering after her, but since his position prevented such aimless ambulations, the most he could do was secretly pour his thoughts into letters. These he concealed from the view of others and usually had delivered to Teishi's ladies-in-waiting through Ukon no Naishi.

The more the empress consort studied the dignified beauty of the new prince's face, the more he seemed the very image of the emperor when he had been a child. She often dampened her sleeve with tears, thinking, "Alas, if only the former times had continued." Korechika prayed to the gods and buddhas with single-minded devotion, thinking that if only this prince could grow up healthy, their clan's former glory would again shine.

The younger brother, Takaie, though reared in the same family, possessed a certain political discernment and was able to see the whole situation objectively from a broad perspective. In this respect he was more like Michinaga than like his father or elder brother. Even if Prince Atsuyasu should safely reach maturity and be endowed with intelligence and courage, it was clear to Takaie that as long as his uncle, Michinaga, enjoyed a long life and remained in power, the clouds gathering over their clan would only grow thicker, never to be penetrated by a ray of sunlight. The depth of the emperor's feelings would not matter —or rather might even prove to be a liability to the former regent's household. Takaie had learned a lesson from the setback of exile and had shed the presumptuousness of a willful, indulged child. He had turned into a self-possessed, dignified young man with both a far stronger sense of pride in himself and a keen discernment. In that respect he stood in remarkable contrast to his elder brother, Korechika, whose exuberant wit and charm had so shone when all was going favorably, but who, since his fall from power, had turned into a weak-willed, mediocre sort of person confined to effeminate querulousness, relying for future prospects only on hopeful observations and placing blind faith in the power of incantations and prayers. Rather than sympathizing with his own elder brother, Takaie was often seized by a desire to spurn him.

Empress Consort Teishi, on the other hand, was quite different from Korechika. In Takaie's eyes, she seemed to radiate a far more finely honed wisdom than she had had even during the zenith of her salon in the imperial women's quarters, where she had enjoyed status as the only empress. The cares that come with age—combined with having borne two children—had left her thin and fragile in appearance, as if her body were but a cast-off shell with only thick black hair appearing above mounds of clothing. Even so, an inviolable noble purity resided in the almost translucent white of her bosom, like moonlight on snow in the depth of winter.

"No matter how they try to smother the emperor's feelings, he'll still fly to the empress consort. That's something that Michinaga can't change no matter how he decks out the child empress." When there were no letters from the emperor for two or three days, Takaie would make such a remark as if to deride his elder brother's fretting. Korechika somehow felt relieved to hear his younger brother speak so confidently.

Empress Consort Teishi had come to love the emperor with a deep love held mutually and equally. It was a love distinct from the natural maternal affection she had for the young prince and princess. In a roundabout manner, the emperor evaded Michinaga's zealous efforts to focus his affections on the new empress and remained passionately attached to Teishi. The empress consort basked in the warmth of his devotion. For her, it was a far more secure feeling than she had experienced during their early years together, when they were innocently amusing themselves with music and games in what seemed like a never-ending, halcyon spring day. It was after falling into adverse circumstances that she was truly able to appreciate the gravity and intensity of the emperor's love. Though in actual life she had been reduced to circumstances unworthy of her status, her heart was yet nourished by these newly realized feelings, and she was unable to think of herself as having been abandoned.

In *The Pillow Book*, Sei Shōnagon never seems to portray her noble mistress in a state of dejection; rather, the Empress Consort Teishi depicted there is a woman always surrounded by a bright aura. To dismiss Sei Shōnagon's description as mere idealization, however, would also be a biased view. Even after she had fallen into unfavorable circumstances, the empress consort's beauty and nobility of character increased in radiance. According to *A Tale of False Fortunes*, a refined atmosphere permeated her quarters in spite of the fact that materially her life stood in pathetic contrast to what she had formerly enjoyed in the court.

One time when Takaie visited Narimasa's residence, Teishi was sitting at a desk within the curtained dais writing something. When she suddenly looked up, he could guess from the gleam in her eyes and the maidenly rosiness of her cheeks that she must be writing a reply to one of the emperor's letters.

"Am I bothering you?"

She shook her head and had Kureha bring a cushion. Then she emerged from within the curtains and took her seat in the main hall.

Takaie watched Kureha withdraw to do as she had been bidden. "That lady-in-waiting has been with you for a long time, hasn't she? If I'm not mistaken, I believe she was in your service even before I went to Tajima."

Teishi nodded. "That's right. I suppose it has been six or seven years now. Even in the fire at the Nijō mansion when you two were away, she risked her very life to protect me. We were about to be burned alive."

The dreadful scene of the Nijō mansion engulfed in flames appeared vividly before her eyes, like a painting of hell. She had been at the time only half-conscious, but she was vaguely aware that someone tried somehow to lure her into the flames, and that someone else headed the villain off and saved her by taking her outside. She was informed later that the one who had saved her was Secretary of the Imperial Police Yukikuni, but apparently the sole witness to the life-and-death struggle was Kureha, who had never said a word about the incident. Moreover, Teishi never asked.

When she thought about it, Teishi realized how very fortunate she was to have been able to give birth to a healthy princess after experiencing such danger during pregnancy. And again, it seemed that it was after she had passed through those dangerous flames that something heavy—something she did not quite understand herself—sank into her soul, making it resistant to all caprices that would move it.

After Kureha had gone from sight, Takaie continued to stare in that direction and said, "So, then, she's loyal to you I suppose, that lady-in-waiting. . . .What is her background? Somehow I don't like the look in her eyes."

"Ho, ho." The empress consort laughed merrily behind her fan. "I'm no match for you. His majesty also says that Kureha's eyes are like those of an *Asura* child. But as for myself, I would rather have someone whose eyes show character than a woman whose eyes conceal their expression behind narrow slits. . . ."

Takaie said, as if to himself, "They have a sinister light about them . . . those eyes. . . . It seems that someone like you ought to have noticed that."

The empress consort smiled lightly and said, "Sinister, you say? When a woman is in love, she becomes very suspicious, you know."

"She has a lover? . . .Who is it?"

"I don't know for certain, but I hear that it is Yukikuni, of the imperial police."

"He's the officer who saved you from the fire, isn't he?"

"That's right. Some of the servants have said that she is feeling dejected because he won't take her as his wife, even though they've been lovers for rather a long time."

"Hmmm." Takaie folded his arms as if lost in thought.

"Why are you concerned about a fledgling lady-in-waiting like her? It's unbecoming for you to . . ."

"No, I don't really have any ground for thinking so, but

. . . if she's so in love with this Yukikuni, wouldn't it be better to have them marry and let her leave your service? You'll be returning to the palace again soon anyway, and . . . I just don't want that woman to be at your side."

"If it seemed that she would become Yukikuni's wife, I would be only too happy to give her leave, but . . ." Teishi seemed to be absorbed in thought for a moment, and then added, "Just what are you thinking that my return to court will be like, anyway? The lady of the Fujitsubo Pavilion will be away, and his majesty is anxious to have me return during her absence, but I'm sure that a lot of troublesome things would come up again. . . ."

"Was there something to that effect in his majesty's letters? I have heard a few things from other sources. . . ."

"What kind of things have you heard?" The empress consort asked as she leaned one elbow against an armrest.

"I heard that his majesty has told the regent he wishes to abdicate soon. They say the regent dissuaded him, saying such a thing was preposterous, and that the empress dowager then proposed you come to the palace."

"Actually, it was in response to that very thing that I was just now writing a letter. I told his majesty that he must not do anything childish and make trouble for the lord regent."

Takaie laughed with delight. "Well, now, you've become rather good at tormenting the emperor, too. You're quite grown up now, aren't you? As for strategies now to keep the regent in check, even I think the best thing is for his majesty to say that he wishes to abdicate. After the regent has gone to the trouble of presenting the lady of the Fujitsubo Pavilion at court and even making her empress, a thirteen-year-old consort of course won't be able to produce a prince for a while yet. The crown prince is older than his cousin, the emperor, and already has princes by the lady of the Sen'yōden Palace. If his majesty were to abdicate now, our uncle would not be able to assert his authority as a maternal relative, and if he is not able to keep his majesty on the throne for at least ten more years, everything he has so carefully arranged will come to nothing."

"Yes, but . . . his majesty's feelings are not merely a matter of bargaining. He seems to have become truly weary of always being afraid of offending this person or that, and of not being able to live freely and without constraint, as he would like."

"That's because he is unable to see your face whenever he wants to. Since you live apart, he hears nothing but unpleasant things." What Takaie was referring to was the time recently when the empress consort had departed from the palace, and the officials who ought to have accompanied her were not available because they were all clamoring to attend Michinaga on his trip to Uji. The emperor had been displeased that his beloved empress consort and prince should be subjected to such rude treatment.

"I mustn't let such things bother me. Even his majesty wrote a letter urging me to forget about the matter."

"That's because you occupy the position of victor," Takaie said with a laugh.

"How am I a victor? I'm the very incarnation of Po Chü-i's line, 'The sun sets on a forlorn shadow.'"

"No, I don't think so at all. Both Korechika and I lost miserably in our battle with our uncle, but you alone have won. His best efforts, even presenting his virgin daughter at court, could not succeed in wresting his majesty's affections away from you. . . ."

"I wouldn't be so sure. The lady of the Fujitsubo Pavilion may still be very young, but I think she has the ability eventually to capture his majesty's feelings."

"In the future, I suppose. But you know, now that I think about it, after our father died five years ago, you did the right thing in refraining from putting too much pressure on the emperor to appoint our brother as regent. At that time you were the only one able to resist the empress dowager. And yet, if you had done so you might have become another power-hungry noblewoman, like Yang Kuei-fei or Empress Wei of T'ang, but you surely would not be able to experience the joy that's yours now of believing in the love of just one person, no matter how lonely and defenseless you might be. You sacrificed our family's glory and clung steadfastly to that one person's sincere devotion."

"That may be true," Teishi nodded compliantly. It would only seem disagreeable to assume a false humility in front of her keenly perceptive younger brother. "Of all the happiness in this world, I don't really know which is the greatest. But I don't think, as our older brother and our nurses do, that the past was happy and that our present circumstances are unhappy. There are times when I think about the little prince and princess and wonder how it would be if our father were still alive. But then, we all have our various fates, and we can't extricate ourselves from them by our own power. Even though I've never talked about such feelings, I suppose that the only one who really understands them is Shōnagon [Sei Shōnagon], who is often despised as being too forward." Then the empress consort smiled calmly and added, "It seems lately that my body has grown considerably weaker, and I have no idea when I shall leave this world. But even after I die, I at least do not intend to become an evil spirit full of cursings and malice toward others. You'll probably live a long life, so after I'm gone, please see how things go, all right?"

Takie answered, laughing, "I understand. I don't believe that you have that sort of vindictiveness in you either."

Not many days after this conversation had taken place, Kureha disappeared from Narimasa's mansion without saying a word to anyone. Since her clothing and personal effects had been left as they were, it was rumored among the ladies-in-waiting attending the empress consort that perhaps she had been spirited off. Teishi herself surmised, however, that Kureha probably had eavesdropped on her conversation with Takaie and decided of her own accord to leave.

"Wouldn't she have gone into hiding at the house of Imperial Police Yukikuni? Yukikuni comes to this house occasionally to do guard service for your highness. Shall we try asking him?" Though quite out of character for him, the master of the house, Narimasa, made this suggestion, having heard all of the rumors about the love affair. The empress consort, however, told him just to leave the matter alone and made no attempt to have Kureha's whereabouts investigated.

Soon after that, at the urging both of the Higashisanjō empress dowager and Michinaga, Teishi took the prince and princess and returned to court, presenting herself at the apartments of the empress' household.

The Fujitsubo empress had left to visit her parental home, and the emperor was able without reservation to shower his affection on the empress consort and to dote upon Prince Atsuyasu even more than he had done for the first princess.

The empress consort had become much thinner than the last time she had returned to the Nijō mansion. She had such a fragile appearance about her that it seemed as if she might melt away if one were to embrace her. There was not a trace, however, of any concealed melancholy, and she appeared genuinely to enjoy being with the emperor.

One spring evening, when the cherry trees in the front garden were in spectacular bloom, the emperor summoned Teishi to his daytime quarters where he played his favorite flute to the accompaniment of her Japanese *koto*. Cherry blossoms were scattering thick and fast in the breeze, and some petals came fluttering inside the bamboo blinds from beyond the balustrade. They landed on Teishi's glossy black hair and on her quickly moving, slender fingers, darting across the strings like white fish as she played her *koto*.

Just then, Michinaga was sauntering along the veranda. When he came to the corner of the balustrade he sent his attendant back and drew closer to the bamboo blind in order to listen to the performance without interference. There he became absorbed in the music. Not having heard the sound of the empress consort's *koto* for some time, Michinaga was surprised at what a clear, wonderful tone her fingers drew from the strings. What agitated his heart, though, were the clearly differentiated feelings of pensive melancholy and suddenly soaring joy in the tone of the emperor's flute, quite different from anything Michinaga had heard in the Fujitsubo Pavilion. Had he been an uncouth type ignorant of music, Michinaga would probably have felt nothing at hearing this performance, but his own accomplishment at both the *koto* and the flute made him very perceptive to the supreme bliss of the emperor's and

Empress Consort Teishi's exclusive love for one another, as expressed in the music they made together.

"Well, your excellency, what are you doing standing outside in a place like that?" When a lady-in-waiting to the emperor crossed the connecting corridor and addressed him in a surprised tone, Michinaga was startled out of his complex state of mind. He answered good-naturedly, "Shh, be quiet! The performance by the emperor and empress consort is interesting, and I'm trying to listen secretly."

At that, the music inside stopped abruptly, and the emperor's voice could be heard to say, "Has the regent come . . . here?"

> Michinaga entered the room, and Teishi drew a curtain toward her, partially concealing herself. She did not retreat deeply within the curtains, however, and on her smoothly flowing hair, with not so much as a single strand out of place, scattered cherry blossom petals could be seen, like chips of gilding on a lacquered box. Over a robe as white as maidenflower blossoms she wore an overgarment of light green. Her crimson divided skirt spread out before her, giving her an extraordinarily refined appearance. Even to the Lord Regent's eyes, which had seen and compared countless women of high rank—including, of course, his own sister, the Empress Dowager—the Empress Consort seemed infinitely more graceful and charming, and he did not wonder that the Emperor should be madly in love with her. Michinaga's own daughter, whom he was accustomed to seeing as well-featured in her childhood, seemed immature by comparison. If only Teishi were not on the scene, then in five or six years His Majesty's heart would begin to soften and he would become intimate with the Regent's daughter. But now Teishi quite occupied the Emperor's august heart, and the two of them were able to perform music together happily and quite naturally. However, it was after this time that a plan formed in the Regent's mind to move the Empress Consort out of the way.

In this manner, *A Tale of False Fortunes* relates the immediate cause of Michinaga's initial concoction of a second strategy.

Chapter Six ⌢

As Empress Consort Teishi continued to live at court with the emperor, once again her periods stopped and she became violently ill with morning sickness. She grew thin, and it was decided at the end of the third month that she should return to Imperial Steward Narimasa's house. The emperor felt apprehensive about having her and his children stay there long and tried to arrange for them to stay at the Sanjō mansion belonging to the empress dowager, but he was unable to do so.

Even in appointing stewards or priests to perform prayers, the emperor knew there would be many requests from the empress consort to which he would not respond for fear of offending Michinaga. He enlisted the services of a certain priest on whom he had relied since childhood and ordered incantations and prayers, hoping anxiously that all would go according to plan. It was all very different from either of the previous births.

In spite of all this, the empress consort maintained a cheerful appearance. She seemed, nevertheless, as fragile as a flower beaten by the rain. At the sight of her, the emperor was plagued by the inescapable anxiety that this might turn out to be the ultimate parting. He wanted to summon Korechika and Takaie to ask that they keep an attentive watch over their sister and her children, but he restrained himself, realizing that summoning them to his presence after their return from exile—and having had no public dealings with them otherwise—would only be worse in the long run for the empress consort.

With the return of the young empress to the palace that summer, the Fujitsubo Pavilion was suddenly bustling with activity. Such events as the Star Festival and the moon-viewing banquets were celebrated in a more spectacular manner than usual, with poetry and music to grace the festivities. However, at about the time autumn winds began to blow, the new empress complained that she did not feel well; she had a fever and seemed to be in distress. Michinaga and everyone in her service treated it as a matter of grave concern to the whole realm and spared no effort in caring for her, calling on doctors and commissioning incantations and prayers.

The emperor also went to the Fujitsubo Pavilion daily to inquire after her condition. Ordinarily she seemed older than her actual years, but in her illness she cried like a little girl, saying she wanted to go home. At such times she seemed so very juvenile and pitiable to the emperor.

Here again, an evil spirit appeared to be taking advantage of her weakened condition, haunting her bedchamber and obstructing her recovery. The late grandfather of the empress consort, Takashina no Naritada, had turned into a most dreadful ghost, raging furiously about the altar where rites were being performed for the empress' recovery. A young boy not yet wearing a court cap was possessed by this spirit. His voice was hoarse, but it had the power of a grown man, and freely mixed into the curses he uttered were phrases reflecting both Chinese and Japanese erudition. The ghost's relentless cursings and denunciations seemed to horrify Michinaga, who actually had known Naritada.

In reality, though, it was not clear whether this ghost of Naritada was genuine or merely a fraud devised by a living person. According to the author of *A Tale of False Fortunes,* a politician of Michinaga's stature can, without so much as moving a finger, weave into the cumulative fabric of events strange tricks that would never occur to an ordinary person, and thereby easily turn things to his own advantage.

Eventually, another spirit would appear that had the manners and speech of the empress consort, but according to *A Tale of False Fortunes,* it was not Teishi's living ghost. It was, rather, a reenactment of the role Ayame of Miwa had played some years earlier when the empress dowager was suffering such distress. After that incident, Ayame had left the empress dowager's service and had spent her time either rusticating at the old nun's cottage or serving at Michinaga's residence, the Tsuchimikado Palace. Since then, she was estranged from her sister, Kureha, and the two had not seen each other for two or three years.

Kureha had come to the nun's cottage in about the sixth month. After suffering for half a month through the chills and fevers of what seemed to be a case of ague, she sent a letter to her elder sister expressing a desire to meet. Ayame accordingly set out without delay to the nun's place near the North Mountain.

Kureha was lying down in an inner room. Ayame was surprised to see that her sister's once-youthful cheeks—normally so plump and with a vermilion-like ruddiness about them—were now hollow and wan, as if she had just been exhumed from a grave.

"I was shocked to hear of your illness and came to see you. After your scathing denunciation of me some years ago, I haven't felt worthy to call myself your sister, but not a day has gone by since then that I haven't thought of you. Mother asked us to stay close throughout our lives. I'm happy that my heart's wish has been fulfilled, and we can meet like this. . . ." She took her younger sister's emaciated hand in her own, and tears trickled down her cheeks as she spoke.

Kureha's sunken eyes now appeared even larger; she fixed them on her sister and said with labored breath, "Ayame, it was childish of me to have become angry at you then, and I am truly sorry. I'm no longer in the empress consort's service. I have also been abandoned by Yukikuni and have nothing more to live for."

"Well! What happened? . . . Did the empress consort perhaps find out that you are my sister, and grew cool toward you? . . . Or did someone else in her service slander you?"

"No, no. Her highness did not suspect me in the least. It was my decision to turn my back on her kindness."

The immediate cause of Kureha's illness was the rift that had grown between her and Yukikuni. Deep beneath it was an agony born of the strong malice toward the empress consort, whom she had served with such love and esteem since childhood.

Some time previously, when Kureha had eavesdropped on the conversation between Takaie and the empress consort and realized that Takaie saw through her, something awoke in her heart, as if a small serpent that had been slumbering there suddenly lifted its head for the first time.

Perhaps it came from a vindictiveness smoldering in her heart, like billowing smoke from the night of the conflagration at the Nijō mansion when Yukikuni, in his ardor to save the empress, shook off Kureha's hand and left her in the flames. Until that time she had worshipped the empress consort as if she were an incarnate bodhisattva and had sympathized with her in all of her disappointments. It was because of Kureha's single-minded adoration of her mistress that she had cut off relations with her own sister. When such strong feelings of devotion were overturned, their place was taken by a horrible, burning obsession, turning into a hatred that secretly cursed Empress Consort Teishi.

Yukikuni vaguely sensed the cause of Kureha's anger and renewed his love affair with her in an attempt to placate her. Yet there remained indelibly in his senses the memory of having gathered the peerlessly beautiful empress consort into his arms in the middle of those flames, and having felt her cold black hair and her skin, moist as flower petals. Though he thought to assuage Kureha's anger and perhaps take her to wife, his heart recoiled in disappointment every time he saw her face. In the end, his regret at having renewed his love affair with her on that one night at Hase grew only deeper.

Nevertheless, Yukikuni genuinely feared Kureha's tenacity, and on the surface he showed no sign of disliking her. But when she left the empress consort's service without saying a word to anyone and sought refuge in his house, his patience turned into irrepressible anger, and he roundly reproached her.

"In no way can I condone your stealing away unannounced from the empress consort's palace. If the former regent were still in power, I might have been willing to overlook such an indiscretion and not condemned you too harshly. But as you are fully aware, the empress consort's quarters have lost to the Fujitsubo Pavilion, and she has sunk into wretched circumstances.

Imagine how deeply hurt she must be if someone like you suddenly disappears from her retinue. I never again want to see someone like you who has betrayed the empress consort.... Well, enough of that. If you return immediately to Sanjō and if you continue your service as you have up to this time, after six months or a year I'll take you as my wife and you may live here." By threats and intimations Yukikuni tried to convince Kureha, but she was not her usual submissive self. She fixed her large, piercing eyes on him as if she could see to the bottom of his heart and, after a long silence, said without so much as shedding a tear, "Enough of your lies! Ever since the fire at the Nijō mansion I have known very well that you do not love me. You feel for the empress consort a passion that can never be realized, and you despise me. Oh, my foolishness for having been drawn on by a lingering attachment to you! Even if I see no other way for myself but death, I can't go on oblivious to your deceit. This is good-bye, both to her highness and to you." With that, she turned her back and left, never once looking back.

From that moment Kureha's attachment to Yukikuni turned into an uncanny, vengeful desire to curse the empress consort.

Kureha ordinarily desired to be compliant, and such an aberrant obsession caused a sore festering of her natural urges. This inevitably resulted in a fever, and within one month's time she had wasted away to a mere shadow: an appalling, spider-like metamorphosis.

When she determined to meet with Ayame, Kureha had arrived at a certain conclusion after battling her illness and her inner turmoil: "I have only one motive in wanting to meet with you, sister. If his lordship the regent tries to have you act as a false medium, as he did once before, I would like to have him use me to play that role."

"What! ... Weren't you the one who so despised me then for my imitation of the empress consort that you would have nothing to do with me? ... And now ... why?" Ayame had heard only that the love affair between Yukikuni and Kureha had been broken, but she knew nothing of Yukikuni's secret love for Empress Consort Teishi. She rather doubted she had heard correctly the words issuing from her sister's mouth. It was all the more incredible because she knew Kureha had served Empress Consort Teishi with a love and esteem that went beyond a mere mistress-servant relationship. Ayame was unable to fathom this sudden reversal of her sister's feelings.

In an attempt to allay her sister's doubts, Kureha offered the following explanation for her motives:

Actually, it was only as long as she cherished the hope of bringing her love affair with Yukikuni to consummation that she had remained in service to the ill-fated empress consort. Such service was beset by numerous insufficiencies and causes for depression, and Kureha could no longer endure it. It was through the good offices of Michinaga that she and Ayame had come to serve at court in the first place, and she wanted to enter into a service that would be worthy of his notice and hoped that sometime in the future he would introduce her to a man—it did not really matter what his rank or lineage might be—who could assure her an abundant life.

Ayame appeared to accept both the mysterious reversal of Kureha's feelings and the striking change in her countenance as the inevitable result of a young woman's disappointment in love. The empress' illness and the evil spirit obstructing her recovery immediately came to mind. Though Ayame was not attuned to Michinaga's way of thinking, it seemed to her that the ruse of using the empress consort's vengeful spirit to torment the empress had not been adopted because she had broken ties with Kureha and had no way of knowing the intimate details of the empress consort's mannerisms. There was no one else suitable to act as a medium. It occurred to Ayame that her younger sister's offer might please the lord regent, and she left the nun's cottage determined to report this to his excellency.

Rumors spread throughout the women's quarters that the new Fujitsubo empress was being tormented by a woman's spirit whose identity was uncertain.

The reports were soon recounted to the emperor by the nurse Tō Sanmi, whose tone intimated it was the living ghost of the empress consort. The emperor was stunned. Though only once, he had vividly seen the living ghost of Empress Teishi when the Higashisanjō empress dowager had been ill. When he met with Teishi after that his fears had vanished, but now they were living apart from one another. It did not seem unreasonable to him that an uncanny resentment should smolder in the unrelieved gloom of her mind, or that this should turn into a tenacious obsession toward the new empress, her rival in love and the virginal daughter of the man who had toppled her from power. Such suspicions were bolstered by rumors that ghosts stalked Imperial Steward Narimasa's house on Sanjō.

But no! He could not imagine that Teishi of all people would conceal such hateful feelings. Prior to leaving the palace she had become even more fragile and thin than before, having the appearance of a rain-soaked hibiscus blossom whose petals were unlikely to last till the morrow. Even then, she did not show the slightest sign of agitation, and when he had taken her in his embrace, he felt as if he were adrift in a scented mist. She did not even petition him concerning Prince Atsuyasu's future. It was as if she had wrapped him in a thick, protective care far deeper than maternal affection. Properly speaking, it was he who should have been protecting her, and yet even in her adverse circumstances she took care to make certain that no animosities should arise between him and the regent. How could someone with such a clear, pure heart harbor that kind of fury toward the young new empress, becoming a living ghost and attacking her on her sickbed?

His majesty continued to deny that it was Teishi's living ghost attacking the empress, but the rumors persisted. Daily, a lady-in-waiting or servant in his retinue would hesitantly relay the latest gossip.

Nothing definite was said about the identity of the living ghost, but it was plainly implied that it could be none other than the empress consort. The night before last, the possessed lady-in-waiting stole into the curtained dais where the empress was sleeping, pulled her hair, and tried to beat her. At that point a priest used his rosary to whip the possessed woman into submission. Although they had moved the empress' room to the north side and were constantly performing the five altar rites, yesterday the evil spirit possessed a medium whom the regent had called in. She continued to spew out horrible curses and denunciations, saying that unless the new empress shaved her head in renunciation of the world and withdrew from the court, her very life would be in danger. They reported that even Michinaga was at his wit's end and considered taking the empress to his Tsuchimikado Palace. He resisted his wife's entreaties to do so, however, concluding that such a tenacious spirit would not be deterred by such a move. The emperor thought to visit the empress at her sickbed, but Michinaga headed off that possibility. His Majesty said, "Is the empress' condition still not improving at all? I should like to pay her a visit." Michinaga answered casually, "No, it would be better if your majesty did not go. Many reputable monks, including the abbot of a temple, are praying on her behalf, and she will no doubt soon recover." With that, he shifted the discussion to some legal matters requiring imperial sanction. Michinaga always took meticulous care that his majesty not worry for a moment. The emperor felt he could rely on such an uncle as regent, but somehow he detected in Michinaga's good-natured countenance a concern for more than just the empress' illness.

The emperor asked anxiously, "It has been rumored that some unidentified evil spirit is plaguing the empress. . . . I can't imagine that she would be the object of such spite." Michinaga immediately recognized in the emperor's wrinkled brow a worry exceeding words. "Who told you such things? I have sternly commanded everyone not to say anything to your majesty that would upset you. What you have heard is sheer nonsense." He offered no further explanation.

The rumors also spread to the empress consort, who was living in seclusion at the house of Imperial Steward Narimasa in Sanjō. It was Korechika who informed her of the gossip. He intimated that, even if Teishi's spirit unconsciously possessed the new empress and obstructed her recovery, it was only what she deserved. The empress consort appeared deeply hurt to hear of the rumors. She made no reply, but just glared with contempt at her elder brother, who of late had suddenly grown quite plump and even seemed to have trouble getting up from his seat, a condition unbecoming for his age.

When Takaie called on her the following day, she brought up the matter herself and vehemently denied that she had anything to do with it.

It was the middle of an autumn month, and the face of the moon appeared bright. Though nothing compared to the palace grounds, in the untended front garden of the Sanjō mansion dew-drenched bellflowers and wild pinks were blooming among the heads of eulalia. From the garden a chorus of insects could be heard, creating an enchanting scene.

Teishi leaned against an armrest near the bamboo blinds, listening to the insects. When she looked up at Takaie's face, her countenance rivaled the clarity of the moon. "Have you heard the rumor that my living ghost has become an evil spirit and is tormenting the Fujitsubo empress?"

"Yes, I've heard it," Takaie answered nonchalantly, as if he thought the matter of no import.

"I heard yesterday. When Korechika told me about it, it was the first I had heard anything. . . ." The empress consort closed her eyes and was silent for a time, as if listening intently to a voice deep within her own heart. The moonlight bathed her eyelids in a bluish light, and to Takaie they looked like large flower petals.

"I simply cannot think that my own spirit could be stalking the Fujitsubo Pavilion. They say that, even if you are unaware of it in your waking consciousness, a spirit traverses dream and reality, but I have never seen anyone like the Fujitsubo empress even in a dream, much less do I recall ever having expressed spite toward her or cursed her. . . . Even when I was at the palace, I never once went to the Fujitsubo Pavilion, and I have no idea what the place looks like."

"Hah!" Takaie burst out laughing. "Even an empress gets lost sometimes, it seems! This whole thing is a silly invention. I'm suspicious even of the claim about our grandfather's spirit. There, now, you should just dismiss all of this as grand-scale theatrics contrived by the regent in order to manipulate the emperor. . . ."

"Theatrics, you say? . . . What does that mean?"

"I mean, it's all a farce aimed at tearing his majesty's heart from its attachment to you. Well, now, why don't you just try to forget about the matter? The emperor is wise, and he'll be sure to see their true forms under their stage makeup."

"Do such things really happen?" The empress consort muttered to herself, half in doubt.

Rumors of the malignant spirit increased daily.

One day the emperor said to Ō Myōbu, the daughter of Tō Sanmi, "Myōbu, I can't persuade the regent to take me to the Fujitsubo Pavilion. But, besides paying a get-well visit to the empress, I'd like to see this malignant spirit without anyone knowing about it. I hear the empress consort at Sanjō is in a precarious physical condition, too, and if she should happen to hear of these rumors, one can only imagine how painful it would be to her. . . . Others might not be certain, but if I see this with my own eyes, I'll know at a glance whether or not it is the empress consort's spirit. If it is the spirit of another woman— or some other evil spirit possessing her—efforts to exorcise it could possibly harm the empress consort, who is with child. I understand that it would be complicated for me to go there officially and openly, but couldn't you and your mother somehow devise a way to get me into the Fujitsubo Pavilion in secret?"

"With all due respect, your majesty." Myōbu, who was a personal servant to the emperor, answered with the familiarity of a foster sister. "Allow me to remind you what would be prudent here, just as my mother would do. If the lord regent were to learn of such an indiscretion, it would not matter that it was at your majesty's command; the blame would be laid upon us. Therefore . . ."

Myōbu answered as if she had no idea how to arrange such a thing, but in reality this command of the emperor's was exactly what she and her mother, Tō Sanmi, wanted to hear. It was not that they felt the least disrespect toward the emperor, but ever since Empress Shōshi's presentation at court, Michinaga had particularly kept his eye on the old nurse and her daughter, and they fervently hoped that somehow or other the emperor's affections would shift from Empress Consort Teishi to the empress alone. For Tō Sanmi, who had raised the emperor from infancy as his nurse, perhaps there was also a touch of jealousy of the emperor's devotion to the empress consort.

At any rate, the emperor's scheme was whispered in detail to Michinaga, who smiled broadly and began ingenious preparations to facilitate the emperor's secret visit.

Two or three days after that, Tō Sanmi presented herself before the Emperor. "This evening, his lordship the regent will return to the Tsuchimikado Palace and will not be staying at the Fujitsubo Pavilion. If your majesty would steal in undetected, you would do well to go there after the first watch. From what I hear from the ladies-in-waiting there, it is precisely at that time that the empress is harassed by the spirit. In the main hall on the east side of the dais priests perform in turns the five altar rites, burning cedar sticks and intoning incantations. No one will notice if you go along the wall curtains from the side door on the west and place yourself outside the main hall. I shall have lady chamberlains and other servants stationed about casually, and if anyone should become suspicious, you could simply say that you were so anxious about the empress' illness that you had come in secret. After you have retired to your bedchamber, I shall come and call for you, so please remain in your court robes."

After the hour of the boar [10:00 P.M.], at the slight raising of the bedchamber curtains as a signal, the emperor slipped out, dressed in a full robe of white patterned cloth and trailing long sleeves. Myōbu, who was waiting there, gently veiled his head with a light garment. They then proceeded from the roofed corridor of the Seiryōden Palace toward the Fujitsubo Pavilion. The emperor was slight, but Tō Sanmi was a large, portly woman. Walking between her and Myōbu, he seemed not to know where he was.

In the front garden swept by the chilly evening winds of autumn, the colors of the flowers had faded. Michinaga had ordered that bell crickets and pine crickets be collected from fields and mountains round about and presented to the empress as an amusement, and these were filling the garden with their chirping. Ordinarily many courtiers would be making their way to the women's quarters to court someone, but now, considering the empress' afflictions, everyone remained on night watch at his own station.

"Kiyonori reporting for night watch!"

As he was walking along the corridor, such distant voices struck the emperor as novel.

People had been cleared out of the way without making their absence appear contrived. Free of the worry of being questioned by anyone, the emperor took his place in the spot prepared for him behind the curtained dais. The room was partitioned by several screens and curtains, with a walled room at the rear. His position offered an optimal vantage: no obstacle in seeing both the main hall and the side room, yet shielded from the opposite view.

The air was thick with the scent of cedar sticks and poppy constantly burning at the altar. Dense smoke was drifting through the room where only the incense fires were blazing red. Mixed with the sounds of the rubbing of rosary beads, of the altar bell, and of exorcists' incantations were the curses and shrieks of the mediums. All of this was radically different from the usual elegant appearance of the palace. The entire hall appeared to be swept in a maelstrom, as if in the fires of hell.

At first the emperor was horrified to see such a scene, but when he peeked inside the curtains he recognized the still child-like face of the empress as she dozed there, her brows slightly drawn together and her splendid black hair laid out on a pillow of Chinese patterned cloth. Tō Sanmi whispered into the Emperor's ear, "The one they are now exorcising is the ghost of Michikane, but this ghost has not been too great an obstruction to the empress' recovery."

Just then, like a tide surging from the main hall toward the side room, a commotion erupted from among the ladies-in-waiting huddled together chanting a mystical Sanskrit formula. From among the long skirts and black hair—which in the dark appeared almost like waves surging against the shore—a dim white figure emerged and stood up as if hoisted. With her cypress-ribbed fan held up against her face, she drew up close to the curtained dais.

"Look! That's it, the way she tilts her head with her neck bent slightly. . . . Doesn't she look like that to you?" Myōbu tugged lightly at the emperor's robe. He did not reply, but appeared to nod deeply within his heart.

There not being two emperors in the land, neither should there be two empresses. Neither will the gods and buddhas allow such a contravention of the laws of society, no matter how much you flaunt your authority. You do not realize that the perverse mind of my father will requite you. . . . Woe, woe!

The lady-in-waiting possessed by the malignant spirit spoke slowly, as if she were chanting a sutra, and then laughed in a resonant, beautiful voice. Jolted awake by that voice the empress raised her head from the pillow, moaned in agony, and threw her head back. "Are you in pain?" "It always strikes at this same time." Her nurse and the senior ladies-in-waiting all spoke at once. They held her in their arms as they pressed down on her chest and rubbed her back. The sight was pathetic to the emperor.

The empress was writhing in pain as if something had seized her at the breast and were pulling her down. The lady-in-waiting possessed by the malignant spirit walked in a swaying manner around the curtained dais with a triumphant look on her face. She continued her cursing in a monotone, as if chanting a sutra, saying this young woman would lose her life in the near future if she remained in the position of empress. When the medium finished her maledictions, a priest whose white brow bespoke much merit accumulated through ascetic practices stepped forward from the altar and stood before the medium.

"What perverse person's spirit is it that comes to curse the empress' future happiness while the entire realm is lamenting her distress?"

"Even if I do not announce myself, it is obvious. . . ."

"No, if you do not announce yourself, there can be no means to placate your enmity."

"Establish the first prince as crown prince. . . . Then this vengeful apparition will disappear."

"Is this the spirit of the departed former regent?"

"No, I am not a man."

"Then are you the ghost of his wife, Kishi?"

"No, no. Why give my mother an undeserved reputation? Don't you realize that this is the living ghost of a pitiful woman, empress in name only, whose makeshift palace is a hut overgrown with dewy weeds, who has been separated from her lord and is passing through a world not quite real, who in spite of herself traverses the distance to this place through darkness and moonlit night?"

Though the voice was not clear, there could be no doubt that it was exactly like Teishi's, tinged with a sorrow like the lingering resonance of a bell cricket's chirp. Watching her as she covered her mouth and drew her black hair into a collar, seeming to avert her face in bashfulness, was like looking at Teishi herself. It gave the emperor gooseflesh in spite of himself.

The empress' distress grew intense and her head was in great pain. Cloths were soaked in a pail of water and placed on her forehead. Her mother, Rinshi, entered through the curtains. The emperor took advantage of the mounting confusion to steal away secretly and return to the Seiryōden Palace along the same route he had come.

He was unable to sleep that entire night. The chilling image never left his eyes: that medium who had wandered in a stupor through the hellish haze of smoke licked by red tongues of fire on the cedar stick altars.

There was something both promising and endearing about her nature which, though exceedingly soft and yielding on the surface, had a tenacious pliancy within, like a twig of green willow that appears easily bent but is difficult to break. Reflecting on that, His Majesty was about to pro-

nounce the rumors true, but was somehow unable to put it into words. Ever since the demise of the late Regent, she must have often despised him as spineless. In various ways she would feign the compassion of a substitute mother in order to keep the world securely in her own grasp, and for that very reason had always refrained from spiteful reproaches. But now that she had become the mother of the First Prince, she showed herself to be like any mother: endowed with a strong, single-minded devotion that would lead her even into tiger or wolf dens. It is not to be wondered, therefore, that she should want to have her son honored as the Lord of All Under Heaven. At any rate, it was strange that the manners, the choice of words, and even the voice of the medium that evening were just like those of the Empress Consort. If such a thing were to become widely known, society would turn against her. . . . No matter how he tried to put such thoughts out of his mind, they continued to vex him, and the night broke without his having slept at all.

The reader has no doubt guessed that, in the confused atmosphere that evening in the Fujitsubo Pavilion, the practiced acting of Kureha of Miwa had created an illusion convincing the emperor that it was the empress consort.

The emperor experienced a profound shock at having witnessed that evening's scene. When his majesty refused to listen to matters of government all the following day, Michinaga knew his plan had worked. He felt assured that if he carried his scheme just one step further, he could succeed in wresting the emperor's heart from its attachment to the empress consort.

The empress consort was growing weaker and was practically bedridden as her pregnancy progressed. This provided Michinaga with a perfect opportunity to spread the rumor that people in semi-invalid states are especially prone to turn into living ghosts and go wandering about.

After several days of studying the expression on the emperor's face, Michinaga approached him. "I have often disregarded your majesty's wishes. The end of the empress' distress is not yet in sight, and her mother has summoned her back home to recuperate at ease. I would like to have your majesty pay her a visit before she departs, and see how she has weakened."

"I, too, had wanted to pay the empress a personal visit and was frustrated because you would not give permission. Well, then, let us visit her at once today."

"A most gracious command! The empress would no doubt be ashamed of the disordered appearance of the pavilion during the day. I shall arrange for you to visit her after dusk." Michinaga returned to the Fujitsubo Pavilion, commanded that the altars for the rites be left as they were, and had the priests continue their prayers. Meanwhile, he had the cluttered side room put in order as much as possible, and then waited for the emperor to arrive.

When the emperor made his appearance after dusk, the empress was sitting up, leaning on an armrest. He felt pity as he looked at her face, which had grown thin and small. And yet it was all the more clear to him then that the feeling he was experiencing was what one would have for a younger sister; it was quite different from the sympathetic pains he felt at seeing Teishi's sufferings.

"I'm happy to see that your color is better than I expected. I should like to visit you every day, but I have restrained myself because your mother is here, and I thought that my presence would only increase her worries. Please get well soon. We have abandoned the *koto* that you started learning with me. You simply must get better so that we can play a game of dice or checkers or something. . . ." The emperor spoke gently as he firmly held the empress' delicate hand and brushed back locks of hair that had fallen over the sides of her face. For her years, Empress Shōshi was a girl of sound disposition, and she thanked the emperor profusely for his visit. Michinaga added that if she went home for a time she would no doubt recover quickly.

The regent's words were interrupted by the nurse's piercing voice. "There! The evil spirit again!" From among a group of ladies-in-waiting near the curtained dais of the main hall, one slipped out as if gliding and grasped the emperor's hand through a part in the curtains.

The emperor was startled and turned to see a lady-in-waiting, her face half covered by her hair, suddenly drawing up to him. She took his hand between both of hers and rubbed her cheek against it.

That gesture was exactly what Teishi did whenever she tried to placate the emperor or ask for something. His majesty was taken aback. It was as if he could sense Teishi's breathing with his own hand grasped between those two cold hands.

The possessed lady-in-waiting, her face buried in the emperor's lap, drew up her long hair and appeared to be weeping bitterly.

Michinaga stopped the attendants as they were about to usher the empress outside the curtained dais, commanding loudly, "Leave her alone! It appears that the evil spirit wants to say something. It's different from other evil spirits. Everyone, withdraw outside the curtains. I am here, and I will not allow any harm to come to the emperor." The nurse and two or three senior ladies-in-waiting prostrated themselves before the empress and, tripping over one another's robes, hurriedly stumbled out into the main hall, where they kept their ears pricked and listened breathlessly for signs of anything occurring within the curtains.

The high-pitched voices of chanting resumed, and along with the swirling dark smoke of the cedar sticks was the heavy odor of burning poppy.

The lamp had gone out, as if absorbed by the darkness, and with only the red blaze from the cedar stick altar as illumination, the emperor was unable to make out the face of the lady-in-waiting possessed by Teishi's spirit. He clearly perceived, however, that Teishi's living ghost had stolen its way into the body of a different woman and was trying to communicate something to him.

"What do you wish to say to me? Please, speak your mind freely. I am satisfied just to hear your voice, even if only for a moment." Forgetting that Michinaga was right there beside him watching, the emperor spoke as he gently shook the back of the lady-in-waiting whose face was buried in his lap. A warm feeling enveloped his whole being, just like the times he had been alone behind the curtains with Teishi.

"Please, listen carefully to what I have to say. While I have continued to pine for your majesty, to this day I have never seen the Fujitsubo empress' face, nor have I been able to visit your majesty. All of the evil spirits up to this point that are said to have been my living ghost were not genuine. Now is the first time I have wandered here, and I shall never again come.

"Your majesty, I have longed for you day and night, but I have never once thought to curse the Fujitsubo empress, who is yet a child. No matter how the Fujitsubo Pavilion flourishes, mine is a happiness unknown to anyone else. I shall feel relieved if your majesty understands just this. Please, do not trouble yourself about me. After I have departed this life, please remember this poem as a keepsake of me. I think that only your majesty knows its meaning."

Upon finishing her declamation, the possessed woman suddenly lifted her face from the emperor's lap and recited twice in a clear and beautiful voice:

> *Yomosugara*   If you do not forget
> *Chigirishi koto o* What we pledged to each other
> *Wasurezuba*   All through that night,
> *Koin namida no*   Then should I like to know the color
> *Iro zo yukashiki*   Of tears born of your longing.*

Thereupon, her feet and hands shook as if they had been doused with water, and she fell prostrate on the spot.

To the emperor, the voice reciting the poem was Teishi's very own: full and splendid but tinged with sorrow. He was absorbed by the poem; reciting it to himself over and over, he once again spread his sleeves like the wings of a great bird, thinking to take her again in his embrace. By then, however, the medium's trem-

---

*It was believed in Heian times that a grieving person might shed tears of blood.

bling body had already been shoved outside the curtained dais, where waiting priests were rubbing their rosaries madly against her bowed head as they chanted incantations of exorcism.

"Your majesty, let your mind be at peace. It was nothing but a groundless rumor that the empress consort's spirit has been pronouncing curses on the Fujitsubo empress. I perceived that to be the case and have not brought your majesty here until now. But the possession we have just witnessed might really have been the living ghost of the Sanjō empress. I know more than anyone that her heart is as beautifully clear as a jewel. Knowing that has been an honor." As he spoke, Michinaga pulled the sleeve of his undergarment out of his overgarment and dabbed his eyes. When the emperor saw that, his tears could no longer be restrained, and his weeping continued until it subsided in sobs.

The emperor's tears were brimming with a supremely pleasant and refreshing sorrow. It appeared to him that Teishi was grieved by his doubts and had sent her living ghost to appear before him.

As if to reawaken that same refreshing sorrow and longing, the next morning a letter to the emperor arrived from Teishi in which the same poem was written in a beautiful, flowing hand. The emperor clasped it to his chest and again melted in tears. It was as if Teishi had softly placed her gentle, thin hand on his convulsing chest, stroking him to calm his heart. "Teishi!" The cry echoed within the emperor's mouth as he grasped her hand in the air before him.

Michinaga's plan had ended up with contrary results. The emperor realized all the more clearly the purity of Teishi's heart, and his loving attachment to her only grew stronger.

The moment the shrewd regent saw that Kureha's acting had failed, he pretended to have seen through her from the very beginning and succeeded in gaining the emperor's trust. Nevertheless, he was deeply angered by the failure of his scheme, and because of his highly obstinate nature, his feelings of indignation only mounted.

Michinaga thought he had been taken in by Kureha. This upstart of a lady-in-waiting had held in contempt the authority of Michinaga, regent and head of the Fujiwara clan. He seethed with anger at her testimony that the heart of the empress consort, a flower shaded from the sun, should be as pure and untainted as a white lotus. His feeling was not merely opposition and hatred toward those who had the nerve to confront him; it was more like the displeasure one must feel at the impertinence of, for example, what one had considered only a harmless worm turning into a snake and biting one's leg, or at the same time at one's own negligence for allowing it to happen.

That same night, Kureha was handed over to the imperial police and was imprisoned for the crime of falsely imitating the living ghost of a person of royal blood and of deceiving the emperor and regent. Her elder sister Ayame was also accused of complicity and was expelled from the empress' palace. About three months later, in the middle of winter, Ayame met Kureha, who had been released from prison in a very wretched state: filthy and with her hair cut short. By that time Empress Consort Teishi, the subject of the false spirit possessions that had controlled Kureha's fate, was no longer in this world.

Death came to Teishi soon after she was delivered of Princess Bishi, the emperor's third child. The first half of the sorrowful passage describing her death is almost the same in both *A Tale of False Fortunes* and *A Tale of Flowering Fortunes*.

The empress consort had grown thinner with the passing months and, not having eaten properly, had gradually grown weaker. Before her delivery her color had turned pale, almost transparent to the bone, much like a silkworm before it spins its cocoon. It was a relatively easy delivery, and on the evening of the fifteenth day of the twelfth month she gave birth to a perfect little princess. Korechika and Takaie were hoping for a second prince and were not entirely satisfied. Before they could celebrate the conclusion of her safe delivery, however, the afterbirth was delayed, her breathing gradually became labored and thinner, and soon stopped altogether.

They had brought hot water, but she would not drink it, and everyone was confused over what to do. They were in a state of panic, and it was particularly worrisome because [the afterbirth] was taking a long time. They brought the lamp closer, and as Korechika looked at her face, he could see no sign of life. Sensing the worst, he touched her only to find that she was cold. In the panic and commotion that followed, the priests wandered about aimlessly, still intent on chanting sutras. Both inside and outside everyone prostrated themselves, wailing loudly, but to no avail. She was gone. Korechika gathered her into his arms and wailed without restraint.

This passage is almost the same in the two accounts, but the part describing the emperor's deep sorrow upon hearing of Teishi's death is much fuller in *A Tale of False Fortunes,* relating in detail feelings of grief and longing not found in *A Tale of Flowering Fortunes.*

From the time he heard that the empress consort's labor had started, his majesty was restless and his mind seemed to be elsewhere. He continually dispatched messengers to the house in Sanjō. At length he was ordering the next one to go before the previous one had returned and was in such a state that by evening he had scarcely eaten anything.

He was relieved to hear of the safe delivery, but somehow remained apprehensive. It was as if a bird of suspicion were still fluttering in his breast. Soon the most sorrowful news arrived. Before even hearing it out, he buried his face in his sleeve and sank onto his armrest, which collapsed underneath him.

"Your majesty! Pull yourself together!" "Please don't let this drive you to distraction!" Tō Sanmi, Ukon no Naishi, and others helped him up, but he only tilted his head limply and made no answer. They summoned the chief court physician and priests to perform incantations. He finally regained his senses after being made to clutch an image of Buddha to his chest and having medicinal tea poured into his mouth. His first words were a moan. "Ah, why could I not have died with her? I hate life!" Then, in a state of utter lethargy, tears welled up from his vacant eyes. Tō Sanmi and Myōbu were sobbing as they wiped his tears.

Before long Michinaga came to pay his respects. Having heard of the empress consort's demise, in spite of the late hour he hurried to the palace to see what state the emperor was in.

"Your majesty, you have my deepest sympathies in your grief." Michinaga put his mouth near the emperor's ear and spoke in a firm voice. He brushed aside Tō Sanmi and the chamberlains, who had been supporting the emperor. His majesty was about to fall over, but Michinaga firmly held him up from behind and grasped his hand.

"Regent, I despise life."

"You mustn't say things so unworthy of your station. The late empress consort would certainly not be pleased to see you so crushed by grief."

"I know... but I can never again touch that soft skin, or have her look at me with those gentle, beautiful eyes ... or wrap that long, cool black hair around me." As the emperor spoke, he stood up totteringly and tried to walk.

Michinaga stepped on the hem of his train and restrained him about the waist, then asked, "Your majesty, what is wrong?"

The emperor twisted to free himself from Michinaga's hands and said in a half-demented voice, "I'm going to Sanjō while her remains are still there. . . . Just once . . . just once I want to touch her face and her hair."

"Your majesty, I sympathize with you! I sympathize with you in your grief, but even when your father passed away, your majesty was not allowed to meet with him. You are the lord of all under heaven, and such rash imperial visits cannot be permitted. That is the uncompromising fate prescribed by your high estate. Otherwise, you cannot maintain your position." After so saying in a forceful voice, Michinaga whispered in the emperor's ear, "I will make sure that your majesty sees the late empress consort's face, but as long as servants are present, please maintain your usual composure." With that, he took the emperor inside the curtained dais, almost carrying him.

"His majesty's grief is such that his face has lost its color. I shall summon priests and have them begin incantations. And tonight I'll remain by his side. Everyone, please, put your minds at ease." With that as a final remark, he entered the curtained dais. Soon he summoned his confidant, a secretary in the ministry of ceremonial, and whispered some command or other to him.

Sometime past midnight, the Lord Regent withdrew and boarded a cart that had drawn up close to the steps of the covered corridor. Pretending he was one of the young nobles attending the Regent, the Emperor was ushered into the cart. He hardly seemed alive as he sat inside, hugging his knees to his chest. They made their way to Imperial Steward Narimasa's house in Sanjō. Michinaga had sent someone ahead with instructions, and the Lord Middle Counselor [Takaie] had managed to keep everything quiet and had not made the Empress Consort's demise public. He arranged it to appear as only a condolence visit by the Regent. His lordship's coming in the middle of the night had been planned in great secrecy, and the ladies-in-waiting continued to weep though they had no more tears; their voices were exhausted, their eyes dimmed, and they were staring straight ahead. All appeared quite dispirited. Only the Empress Consort's younger sister [Mikushige-dono, later concubine to Ichijō] and the Lord Governor-General [Korechika] were within the curtains; the Middle Counselor [Takaie] kept watch outside. At length, the Lord Governor-General said as he prostrated himself with grief, "How gracious of you to come! Just seeing such unprecedented love makes me regret that I cannot trade my own life to bring her back." Michinaga said, "This is certainly unheard of. I was so awed by His Majesty's great love for her that I broke with decorum and brought him here. It is absolutely imperative that you never mention this to anyone. Just arrange for him to see the remains. No matter how strongly he might protest, you should not let him stay long." Thereupon, they brought a lamp and pulled back a section of the curtains for the Emperor to see the remains of the Empress Consort.

Though some time had elapsed since her passing, she had not changed at all. Lying there in august repose, she did not even seem to be a creature of this world, but appeared as noble as if a bodhisattva had assumed the temporary form of an empress. It was especially touching when the Mistress of the Wardrobe [Mikushigedono] stroked the deceased Empress Consort's hair and said through sobs, "His majesty has arrived. Please have an audience with him now." The Emperor shed no tears. As he gazed at her, he could not escape the impression that her spirit must be lingering in her remains. His pain was fathomless.

His time was limited, and he left as if in a dream. The Middle Counselor [Takaie] followed him to the cart and said, "The late Empress Consort herself selected these old letters from among scraps of her usual writing practice and tied them by the cord of the curtain. She must have wanted to make certain that the musings of her lonely, everyday existence would come to Your Majesty's attention. Since they are reminders of the deceased, they are inauspicious, but it must have been the wish of the Empress Consort that you take these back with you and read them." The Emperor nodded vacantly and put the letters in the breast of his robe.

After they returned, the Emperor's mood became somewhat more tranquil, and the Lord Regent's worries were put to rest. At length, the pale light of dawn ended the long winter night.

After retiring to his bedchamber, the Emperor took out Teishi's jottings and read them. He found odds and ends of diaries filled with elliptical accounts of things, but there was not a trace of any bitterness. Among the passages yearning for the Emperor, she wrote that she did not expect to survive the loneliness of this year, a year that had required her utmost circumspection. To that she added the poem of the previous day, and also described her circumstances:

Shiru hito mo	Now is the time
Naki wakareji ni	That I must hasten,
Ima wa tote	Alone and wretched,
Kokorobosoku mo	Down the Path of Parting
Isogitatsu kana	Where all are strangers

Kemuri to mo	Though my body
Kumo to mo naranu	Will not be one of smoke
Minari to mo	Or clouds—
Kusaba no tsuyu o	Remember me when you look
Sore to nagame yo	At dew upon the grass.

They managed to carry out the untimely imperial excursion without anyone finding out, but Michinaga had secretly included the secretary of the imperial police, Yukikuni, among the party that went to pay its condolences. It was necessary to conceal the emperor's grief from outsiders, but among those who were privileged to know, there was an unrestrained and overt display of mourning. Since hearing of the empress consort's demise, it was as if a black curtain had been drawn over Yukikuni's heart. He was unable to confide his feelings to anyone, and his secret grief caused him great anguish of mind.

Through his connections as an official at the Bureau of Imperial Police, Yukikuni learned that Kureha had been arrested for the crime of falsely claiming possession by the empress consort's living ghost, thereby bringing disgrace upon her highness. According to what Yukikuni had heard, keen-eyed Michinaga had seen through Kureha, who, acting out of resentment toward the empress consort, had taken advantage of her knowledge of her highness' voice and mannerisms to feign possession and to curse the Fujitsubo empress. Kureha had been charged with lèse majesté and falsely acting as medium. Those who heard about it praised Michinaga's magnanimous disposition and integrity in taking action to clear the tarnished reputation of the empress consort, who was his own daughter's rival. However, Yukikuni could not help being suspicious about many points in the story.

When Kureha had come to his house for the last time and had broken their relationship, she had not concealed her jealousy toward Empress Consort Teishi and had cursed her very existence. Then, relying on her ties with her sister, Kureha had allied herself with the Michinaga camp and used her thorough knowledge of the empress consort's deportment and words to become a false medium. Yukikuni was also able to sense that it was Michinaga who had made use of Kureha's knowledge. He had used Kureha as a false medium, but then when things had gone awry, he charged her with the crime of lèse majesté while at the same time making a pretense of liberality toward the empress consort. Even those who had firsthand knowledge of his character—a combination of grandiose stateliness with a gentleness that charmed even little girls—would doubtless be unaware of the many tricks hidden in his heart, or of how adroitly he manipulated things. If Yukikuni himself had not felt so keenly an unrequited love for Empress Consort Teishi, he certainly never would have fathomed what was at the bottom of this great politician's shrewd heart.

With all due respect, it must be said that the emperor, the empress dowager, the crown prince, and all courtiers were nothing other than puppets whose strings were controlled by the grand character of Michinaga. How much more, then, were people such as himself and Kureha like insects in Michinaga's eyes, inconsequential creatures that he could let live or kill without so much as moving a finger.

Yukikuni finally realized the true nature of the politics that moved the world. He felt apprehensive about that power, and rather than draw closer to Michinaga, he began unconsciously to cast about for a way to distance himself.

He thought he might go to the eastern provinces. Yukikuni was able to learn something of Taira no Masakado, who, though perishing in the end, had managed to become a local magnate in the eastern provinces and defy the power of the Fujiwaras.

The night after Empress Consort Teishi's death, it so happened that Yukikuni was attending the regent. As he walked along the grand avenue of the capital, he felt as if a fragrance of blossoms penetrated his breast; he mused that the fragrance was like that of the empress consort's robes when he gathered her into his arms in the conflagration at the Nijō mansion. He muttered to himself, "She was the only strong one who did not become entangled in the lord regent's manipulative strings." Though her life had ended in a state of utter loneliness and with no support, Yukikuni could not think of her as a wretched object of pity.

In accordance with the empress consort's often expressed wish, she was buried instead of cremated.

They went to a place about two hundred yards south of Toribeno and there built a mausoleum, surrounded by a roofed wall, to be the resting place of the Empress Consort. Everything was decorated in a very dignified manner. All things had been considered and were taken care of in an extraordinary fashion.

When that evening arrived, the Empress Consort was put into a cart decorated with gold threads. The Lord Governor-General [Korechika] and other nobles of high rank attended the procession. That evening a heavy snow was falling, and the mausoleum where she was to be laid to rest was completely buried. They went and had the snow cleared away, and then put all of the interior furnishings in order. At length, they unyoked the ox, lowered the coffin, and placed it inside. When they were about to leave, all the nobles—including Akinobu and Michinobu—were weeping, utterly distraught. In the meantime, the mausoleum had again vanished beneath the snow. Out of grief, the Middle Counselor [Takaie] recited:

Shirayuki no	No trace remains
Furitsumu nobe wa	On fields deeply blanketed
Ato taete	In the falling snow—
Izuku o haka to	To visit you, how shall we know
Kimi o tazunen	The whereabouts of your grave?

It was all very moving. Would that the events of that night could be painted in a picture and shown to others.

That night, the emperor sat watching the snow pile up in the front garden and would not even enter his bedchamber. When he closed his eyes, he could see vividly Teishi's reclining form, clothed in a dress of white figured cloth and laid within the cart decorated with gold threads, her face and head shaking like that of a living person every time the cart shook, and Korechika and her younger sister steadying her, weeping all the while.

A vision opened to the emperor's mind: after the coffin had been moved into the mausoleum and artificial lotus flowers had been placed around the remains, the lid was placed on the coffin. As the sutra chanting continued, snow fell through the roof, scattering like flower petals on Teishi's remains. It was as if, mingled with those snowflakes, his own love was being scattered over her.

Nobe made mo	Only my heart
Kokoro bakari wa	Traveled to that lone field
Kayoedomo	To pay last respects,
Waga miyuki to wa	But you no doubt were unaware
Shirazu ya aru ran	Of my visit to you.

Steeped in a tranquil sorrow, at daybreak the emperor entered his bedchamber. He dreamed that he was sleeping wrapped in cool, black hair. Upon awakening, he reflected that he must have been recalling that day in his own youth when Teishi had just washed her hair and he had wrapped himself in it before it had dried. He muttered to himself as he pressed his fingers against both of his eyes, "Teishi warned then that I would become the 'frozen emperor,' but now she is the frozen empress. . . ." His heart felt strangely satisfied.

It was about three days after her release from prison that Kureha hanged herself in a pine grove near Empress Consort Teishi's new grave.

During her brief term in prison, she felt deep sorrow for having repaid kindness with enmity by playing the false living ghost of the empress consort. It was rumored that, now that her noble former mistress was in the grave, Kureha was unable to beg her forgiveness, and the "false medium" was no doubt resigned to the fact that there was no other way to expiate so grievous a crime.

After having consummate success as a false medium in deceiving the emperor on the first night, why on the next occasion did Kureha deliver opposite lines, incurring Michinaga's wrath? *A Tale of False Fortunes* gives that account in the last section where Yukikuni—then serving as a samurai near the Iruma River in his native province of Musashi—was out hunting and met Kureha's elder sister, Ayame, among a group of itinerant shrine maidens.

More than thirty years had passed, and both Yukikuni and Ayame were beyond middle age.

Yukikuni despised the likes of shrine maidens as mortal enemies and was about to rout the group of women resting in a field of pampas grass. When he recognized Ayame, he took her to his mansion, gave her clothing, dined with her, and talked with her through the entire night.

The detailed account Yukikuni heard from Ayame was, in fact, an outline of *A Tale of False Fortunes*. It was only then that Yukikuni learned that, on the last evening when Kureha acted as medium, she had prepared her lines in advance, but when she buried her head in Emperor Ichijō's lap, her words stuck in her throat, as if she had become mute. She fell unconscious and did not remember anything at all until she was dragged outside the curtains.

"My sister said before she died that the empress consort's living spirit must have come to the Fujitsubo Pavilion just that once to put the emperor's troubled heart to rest. For my sister, whom you had abandoned and who had betrayed the empress consort, maybe the happiest thing was to hang herself near the mausoleum." Ayame, advanced in years and with sunken eyes, spoke with her shoulders hunched over, warming her hands at the fireplace where the savory aroma of roasting wild fowl was wafting.

"My tendency to single-mindedness when I was young was also the cause of much that I regret. But as I think about it, there would probably be just as much regret even if I had married Kureha and brought her with me to this rustic eastern province, where she would have spent her time around uncouth soldiers, war horses, and farming. The fact that a petty official like myself harbored an unrequited love for the empress consort was the source of both Kureha's and my unhappiness. But, Ayame, you seem to have gotten around a good deal, too. The world and the fortunes of people in it have changed a lot in the more than thirty years since then, haven't they?"

"I live, as you see, the life of a drifter and know nothing of court life, but I do know that the man who was then regent—the one who enjoyed such prosperity and who was lionized by the world as the 'Buddha-Hall Lord'—died not long ago."

"That's right. Two ministers and four imperial consorts came from his family. His strong fortune and confidence in his position in the world was even reflected in a poem he composed:

Kono yo o ba	When I consider
Waga yo to zo omou	That the full moon up above
Mochizuki no	Lacks nothing at all—
Kaketaru koto mo	How like this present world,
Nashi to omoeba	All my very own!

... And then, his eldest daughter, Jōtōmon'in [Empress Shōshi]—that is, the rival to Empress Consort Teishi—has the supreme honor of being the mother of two emperors, Go-Ichijō and Go-Suzaku. But I wonder how happy she was. Emperor Ichijō passed away when he was not much beyond thirty, and though the two princes inherited the throne one after the other, both were sickly and died young. I hear that their mother is now very lonely. When I consider that, I cannot easily forget the personal character of Empress Teishi. In her short life of twenty-five years, she so captivated the emperor's heart. Of all the women of those times, she was the only one able to counter the Buddha-Hall Lord."

When he finished speaking, Yukikuni snapped some pieces from the dwindling supply of firewood and threw them in the fireplace.

The sound of chestnut burrs falling in the grove of trees in back mingled with the sound of falling leaves. Ayame closed her eyes and said nothing as she sat across from Yukikuni. The next morning, she would be reunited with the same group of shrine maidens and journey toward Kōzuke.

A *Tale of False Fortunes* ends with these lines. An investigation of the chronologies reveals that when Michinaga died in the fourth year of Manju (1027), it was still the reign of Emperor Go-Ichijō, so there is some error in dates. But then it is a work of fiction, and perhaps the order of historical events was inverted as a means for its author to suggest something.

About the Author and Translator ~

Enchi Fumiko (1905–1986), the daughter of the noted philologist Ueda Kazutoshi, resolved at the age of nineteen to become a playwright and in 1928 saw the successful staging of her play *Banshun sōya (A Turbulent Night in Late Spring)*. Disappointment in romance, an unhappy marriage, and the Pacific War dampened her literary activity until the appearance of her collection of short stories *Himojii tsukihi (Days of Hunger)* in 1953. Her novels *Onnazaka (The Waiting Years)* and *Onnamen (Masks)* established her reputation as one of the leading writers of post-war Japan.

Roger K. Thomas (Ph.D. 1991, Indiana University) is an associate professor at Illinois State University, where he teaches courses in Japanese language and culture. His research and publications have focused primarily on poetry and poetics of the Edo period (1600–1868), but he maintains an active interest in modern fiction as well and has translated Inoue Yasushi's *Confucius: A Novel*.